I0718742

Odin:

A Paranormal Protector Tale

Book 3 in the Heart of Ice series

DEMELZA CARLTON

DEDICATION

This one is for Carolyn.
Who knew getting kidnapped while trying to write the
story of getting snowed in with Odin would make the
book so much longer?
Definitely not me.
The waffles were worth it, though.

ONE

The sundial in the courtyard greeted Freyja like a nightclub bouncer that wasn't sure she was well dressed enough for tonight's crowd, but was forced by necessity to let her pass anyway.

The feeling was mutual.

The weird, ornate metal sculpture that made absolutely no sense to her, all twisted and jagged, yet somehow able to tell the time. When it wasn't covered in snow, of course. It was supposed to be summer. The archaeology team had already gone up into the mountains to start the dig early, what with the early snowmelt leaving the site bare, but now if it was snowing again, who knew whether they'd be digging or coming back?

Not that she should really be worried about them – they had gear that was rated for Mount Everest, so a small snowstorm in the Jotunheimen Mountains wouldn't be a problem. Karl didn't let a little thing like a blizzard send him home early. The guy was as obsessive about archaeology as her dentist brother was about flossing.

And this time, Karl had already made a discovery so great, they'd called in a helicopter recovery team, which was almost unheard of. Karl insisted a helicopter was only used as a last resort, because of the carbon emissions from the flight and global warming and all, yet he'd called for this one.

Had he really found his iceman? The holy grail of every ice archaeologist?

Saint Nik would be frothing at the mouth if

he had. The shirt he'd found last season was nothing compared to finding the shirt's owner still frozen inside it.

Well, she'd soon find out, when the helicopter arrived.

"We will find it, and we will need you," Karl had said before leaving, like it was some kind of prophecy.

Freyja snorted, just like she'd done then. Prophecies were the stuff of fantasy novels about chosen ones and boys becoming heroes. Not for disgraced doctors who'd never work in a hospital again.

She dug out her phone, wanting to check the message from Lara again. Maybe she should go inside, instead of waiting out here in the cold for the helicopter to arrive.

The phone network access had improved since her last trip up here. Two bars instead of one, though it might drop to zero again if Karl's snowstorm crossed the mountains to here. Her predecessor had told stories about the blizzards up here. Apparently the poor woman had been snowed in for a month when she'd been caught here in an early autumn blizzard. The lab might only be a fifteen minute walk to town in normal weather, but the town may as well be as far away as the moon once the snow started to stick. Or worse, turn to ice.

Funny, that ice was both her bane and her reason for being here at Icelab.

A bog body. An ice mummy. And she'd be the first person to actually see it in its entirety…

All right, maybe Karl's excitement and stubborn certainty had infected her, just like that new virus spreading through so many major cities. She was safer up here, in this isolated laboratory, than back at the main university campus. But if this discovery was so important, surely there should be a team, not just her. What if she did something wrong and damaged the body?

Karl would never forgive her. The academic community would never forgive her. They still hadn't forgiven her for the mistake she hadn't actually made with a patient, almost three years ago, and no one would listen to her now whether it was her fault or not.

Freyja swallowed. One corpse had ended her medical career, but this body might be her redemption. Sure, it was Karl's discovery, but this stranger in the ice could be her salvation. Or…something, at least, to rebuild her career on.

Now she just had to hope he'd been dead for a few centuries, at least, and wasn't some Nazi who'd been running away from the trial for his horrible war crimes.

Then again, if he was a Nazi, no one would care if she made any mistakes dealing with the body.

But he also wouldn't be as big news as Karl was hoping for.

He might not even be a he. Maybe it would be an ice woman.

Take that, scientific community, she thought to herself. What would all those old male academics do if they discovered their holy grail was actually a woman? They'd lose their minds.

An ice mummy, even. Freyja grinned. She'd be calling it that until proven otherwise, and maybe even afterwards. After all, a man mummified in the ice was still a mummy.

She glanced at her watch. She hoped the helicopter would hurry up – she was supposed to video call her mother this afternoon. She'd thought she was running late, but it looked like the chopper wasn't even here yet.

The thumping sound of the blades hit her first – a visceral heartbeat that her own ribs vibrated along with. Only it wasn't coming from the mountains, but from the other direction entirely. What the actual fuck? Had the helicopter not even made it to the dig site yet? Maybe it would've been faster to send the packhorses. Then again, the weight of that much ice would be too much for a horse, surely.

Hence the helicopter was the only option.

The helicopter that was definitely coming in

to land, blowing snow around like it was trying to blast the dirt off the buildings. Even Freyja had to duck back under cover, taking shelter in the lee of a wall that bore a warning sign in three languages, only one of which she was fluent in:

Beware rotor downwash. Do not pass until helicopter has landed.

There was a red line marked on the sign that was hidden somewhere under the layer of snow. Though once the helicopter was done sandblasting (snowblasting?) the place, maybe she'd learn where the line was so she could stay behind it.

When she looked again, the helicopter had landed squarely on the H in the middle of the helipad, the circle now clearly visible. Unfortunately, he'd completely missed the sundial.

The pilot cracked open the door as the rotors slowed.

Freyja grabbed her trolley and trundled it out as best she could through the snow. She hadn't done this since she was a med student on rotation in the Emergency Department, and there'd been a really bad boating accident where they'd literally pulled people out of the water and flown them straight to hospital.

She doubted she'd be doing triage on today's patient, though. Or ever again.

"Sorry I took so long. Had to stop for decontamination first," the pilot shouted as he opened the rear door.

The strong smell of cleaning chemicals leaped out, nearly blinding her.

It must be some new protocol to do with the virus, Freyja decided. At least it was more effective than endless use of hand sanitiser.

"…after delivering the medevac patient," the pilot continued.

Freyja's heart skipped a beat. "One of the expedition team needed medical evacuation? Are they all right?"

The pilot shrugged. "Don't know. Didn't wait around long enough to find out. From what I can gather, he got into a fight with a wolverine, and he didn't win. I could barely fly with the stench, so I stopped for a clean before I came here. You should be thanking me. You can't smell a thing now." He grinned.

Yeah, but that was because the cleaning chemicals had seared her sinuses halfway up to her brain. As long as none of it had touched the ice mummy…

"Who was hurt?"

The pilot shrugged again. "A Dr Free Dolphin or something?"

"Dr Fridolfsen," Freyja corrected. Saint Nik fighting the wildlife. Now that was a new one.

"Maybe," the pilot conceded. "Now, you got anyone else here to do the heavy lifting, or is it just us?"

Freyja grinned. "I'll do it by myself, if you're not strong enough."

Worked every time – on male orderlies, as well as male pilots. No patient ever took more than two people to lift.

Of course, she hadn't counted on this patient being encased in close to a tonne of ice…

After half an hour of huffing, puffing, pulling, pushing and a shitload of swearing, they got the body bag onto the trolley.

It definitely took two of them to wheel it inside, and to transfer the mummy's ice coffin out of the body bag and onto one of the mortuary trolleys with a drip tray for autopsies.

If anyone in med school had told her she'd be doing autopsies for a living, she'd have laughed them out of the university. Now…she still wasn't sure she believed it.

She barely noticed the pilot leaving as she focussed on the mummy. Well, the giant ice block, really, that Karl had assured her contained a person. She'd have to defrost it a bit more before she could confirm it.

Freyja considered taking a couple of preliminary x-rays, just to be sure, then glanced at her watch. No, she'd promised to call her family, and who knew when everyone's rosters would match up again?

The ice mummy could wait. Besides, what if

there were other things frozen in the ice with them, obscuring the x-ray? Rocks, other artefacts, who knew what? Better to wait until more of the ice had melted, so she could get a clearer picture of who this person was.

They'd keep. If Karl was right, they'd waited a thousand years under the ice. A few more hours in the necropsy refrigerator wouldn't hurt them. Not like they'd know.

TWO

"Are you sure you're safe there? Because we would prefer you to be here at home. Doctors are considered essential personnel, you know, even with the borders closed, and your father's been bringing in specialists through the quarantine every week, so we know exactly what to put in your application. With the virus having everyone so scared, hospitals are recruiting like nobody's business. I'm sure they'd even overlook that tiny incident three years ago if you were to apply…" Mum wheedled.

Freyja tried not to grimace. As a bariatric surgeon, Mum's entire career hinged on her optimistic sales pitch that she could deliver weight loss miracles to her patients.

But Freyja didn't believe in miracles – especially not the sort her mother sold. The only doctor jobs back home for her would be as an overworked country GP in the middle of nowhere, or as a public health officer writing endless policy and protocols for the pandemic, every time the WHO issued another update. "No, Mum, it's fine. Healthcare in Norway is every bit as good as it is at home, and I'm probably safer here than I would be on a plane, anyway. I have an entire lab facility to myself, while our fieldwork staff are out at site, and the only people I'll have any contact with are our team for the whole summer. I have more chance of catching some primeval mammoth plague than I have of catching the virus you're so worried about."

Mum opened her mouth to protest.

"Besides, things just got rather interesting here. I can't say much yet, but the team discovered something in the glacier that could be big news. Something I can't wait to work on," she lied. Well, sort of lied. She had to wait until the body defrosted, and she was more nervous than excited about what she might find out when it did.

"Ooh, are you talking to Freyja? Hey, sis. Are you remembering to floss?"

Freyja rolled her eyes. Fintan and his floss. "Oh, yeah, ten times a day. Did you know they sell whalebone floss here? From real baleen whales, because they still hunt whales in Norway. Much better for the environment than plastic, as it's biodegradable, too."

"Wait, did you say you've seen whales while you're in Norway? Oh, please take pictures for me. I heard all the Viking legends about sea monsters are actually whale penis sightings. Krakens and sea serpents and maybe even the

Loch Ness Monster!" Kendall's eyes danced. Trust a urologist to make every conversation about penises.

"I doubt I'll see any whale penises, or any penises, alone in the lab," Freyja said drily.

Kendall's face fell. "None at all? Aren't there any hot Vikings you can take to bed? You are in Norway. I mean, you could always offer them a free prostate check. That's always worked for me."

Of course it had. Kendall flirted as easily as breathing, and male patients were only too happy to have her examine their bits, especially when she made it a habit of cooing over how big and impressive they were.

Freyja couldn't remember the last time she'd seen, let alone handled, a man's…

"No! I don't want to hear about my sister's love life!" Fintan complained, clapping his hands to his ears. "Take care. See you later, sis!"

Mum muttered something Freyja couldn't quite catch, rising from her seat so Kendall could sit down. "Dad said to say he loves you, and to take care. He got called in because of some sort of hospital emergency. A ship with infected people aboard or something. But now everyone else is gone...spill! Have you met any hot guys?"

Freyja shook her head. "I've been really busy with work, and there's no one else here. Even the caretaker quit at the start of the season, and while I heard they'd hired a new guy, I haven't seen him yet. Everyone else is out at an archaeological dig for the summer."

"Yeah, but you can't tell me small towns in Norway are as remote as the ones here in Australia. How far away is the nearest pub?"

"Fifteen to twenty minutes on foot, depending on the depth of the snow," Freyja admitted.

"So what's stopping you from going there tonight and getting some hot Norse cock?" Kendall asked.

"I have a lot of work to do. Like I told Mum..."

Kendall blew a raspberry. "It's the weekend. Universities don't work weekends. You are free to fuck the brains out of whatever hottie you pick up until Monday morning."

"I don't pick up random men in bars," Freyja said.

"No, you don't pick up men anywhere. You're like a nun, you have been since high school."

Freyja sighed. It wasn't her fault she wasn't as clever as the rest of the family. Getting into med school had meant studying way more than Fintan or Kendall, and even then she'd barely scraped in. She'd had no time for messing around with guys, let alone a relationship.

"I want you to promise me something," Kendall began.

"Kendall…"

"Promise me you will go to the pub tonight and have a drink, and a conversation with a man you'd at least consider having steamy hot sex with. Okay?"

"Kendall."

Kendall got that steely look her biggest, toughest male patients knew not to argue with. "I'm worried about you, Freyja. Worried you'll end up all alone with nothing but a herd of cats until you go mad and try to harness them up to a chariot to take you places. Please. Go Norse cock hunting. For me."

Freyja couldn't help it. She burst out laughing. "What would Mum say if she heard you say that?"

Kendall grinned. "She'd shake her head and say she does not want to see the pictures. But I do! Big hairy cock pictures, please!"

Freyja buried her head in her hands. "I am not sending you dick pics."

"Solicited dick pics are totally acceptable. Now, this is what you're going to do. I want you to repeat after me: pub, penis, pictures." Kendall glared into the camera. "Say it!"

Freyja blew out a breath. "Okay, I'll go to the pub. But no promises."

"Yes! Dick pics incoming!' Kendall cheered, before ending the call.

Freyja shook her head. Kendall was right, though. She didn't have anything to do this weekend, while the body defrosted. And when it did, she'd be flat out, running every test she could to work out as much as she could about the person.

Maybe she should go to the pub, just for a little while. And if she met a man she liked, who she'd like even more naked, then maybe…

Maybe.

That was all.

She pulled her coat on, locked up, and headed outside to the garage where she'd parked her car. Of course, the helicopter had blown all the snow up against the roller door, so she'd have to spend an hour or two shovelling to get it out. But there were the two sleek new electric scooters the university had bought…she could squeeze one of them out the snow-free side door, no worries. Plus, instead of leaving her car in the pub car park, she could put the scooter in the boot of the guy's car, if she did find someone worth getting naked with.

Not that she'd be getting naked tonight.

But it might be nice…

Freyja buckled on her helmet, and walked the scooter out into the courtyard before she could second guess herself.

She'd promised Kendall. She'd go to the pub, order a drink and a sausage, take pictures, and then go home. Mission accomplished.

She was a little unsteady at first, almost losing her balance once or twice on the drive to the main road, but as she turned onto the road, she felt confident enough to open up the throttle, to get a little speed. Just as she hit an ice patch. The scooter went flying and so did she, tumbling through the air headed downhill way too fast…until the whole world went white.

THREE

Odin had never been so cold in his life, and he'd fallen into a fjord once when he was ice fishing. This felt like his blood had turned to sleet, but he couldn't even shout for help because he was surrounded by ice. Yet he could move…

He fell a short distance to a floor that was warmer than ice, but not by much. Like he'd fallen out of bed onto flagstones, after waking from a bad nightmare. Only…he'd never had a nightmare quite like this.

He blinked his eyes open, then could not help but stare around the small, square room. All the walls were made of shiny metal, and the ceiling, too. Everything but the floor, which consisted of square flagstones in shiny ice white.

Fuck. Ice. HELP.

Down through the not-ice floor and the earth below, then through snow and actual ice to where the call was coming from.

A woman wearing the most peculiar helmet, buried in a snowdrift.

Odin reached for her, lifting her up.

Her eyes blinked open, blue as a the ice on the fjords in winter…

…and Odin fell in love.

FOUR

Freyja was cold and wet and bumping up and down like she was on a small boat at sea. Which made no sense, because she could have sworn she'd been on a scooter, nowhere near the water…

She forced her eyes open. Yes, she recognised the snow piled up on either side of the road to the lab – she'd driven down here in her car only this morning.

But the bumping?

She squirmed so she could see.

A hard chest that she was pressed against. Bulging arm muscles as the chest's owner carried her.

What kind of man walked around shirtless in the snow?

A man whose grip tightened around her so she didn't fall.

"Must get you inside, somewhere safe and warm, so we can see if you are injured from your fall," he rumbled.

Yes, her fuzzy head agreed. She'd been thrown from her scooter. Might have broken bones or internal injuries. At least she was wearing a helmet…

She patted her head, but all she felt was her own hair.

Well, she had been wearing a helmet. Maybe Dr Hardbody here had removed it, or it had fallen off. As long as it had done its job of protecting her beforehand…

She pointed up the driveway. "Take me to

the lab. We should have everything we need in the first aid room there." And if not, she could always call an ambulance. Karl would have a conniption if she called the helicopter back to airlift her out.

But she didn't think she was that badly hurt. Her pride felt more bruised than the rest of her. Falling off one of the scooters before she'd even made it to the pub for a drink.

Worse, before she met a man worth getting naked with.

Then again, this one was half naked already, and she couldn't deny she liked what she saw. Maybe she did have a head injury.

But with no pain, nausea or dizziness, she'd already made a diagnosis way before they reached the first aid room.

No serious injuries, but in need of dry clothes to prevent hypothermia.

So she directed him to take her to her to the guest room where she'd left her suitcase instead. She stripped off her coat, then her sweater and was about to shuck off her jeans when she realised he was still in the room with her.

And while she'd been undressing, he'd taken off everything.

Holy fuck. All the marble in Rome couldn't hold a candle to him.

This man was made of muscles. Her memory started to name them, like she would have back in med school, but she just shook her head to clear away any unnecessary thoughts. This veritable god of a man was standing here in her bedroom, naked, his enormous cock saluting her with the same eagerness she felt.

Her mouth was dry. "Thank you for saving me from the snow, and carrying me all the way back here. I don't suppose you'd be interested in a night of hot sex as a thank you?"

He frowned. "Are you not injured?"

Freyja slowly shook her head as she stripped off the rest of her clothes. "Nope, not injured. Good to go all night." Oh god, had she said that bit out loud? Because she was. She wanted to climb him like a tree, wrap her legs around those thick thighs and grab his arse with both hands while he fucked her into next week with that monster cock.

So she wrapped her arms around his neck and kissed him with everything she had.

"Fuck me," he breathed, his eyes wide with wonder.

"That's the plan," she replied as he lifted her up.

FIVE

It took every bit of his self control not to spin her around, slam her into the wall and fuck her standing, but this wasn't about a quick release, even if they had just met. No, he intended to adore her all night, if she had the stamina for it, as she said.

So he laid her reverently on the bed, an enormous affair that was more than big enough for the two of them.

Bigger than the bed he'd shared with Frigg, that one time they'd lain together and conceived the twins…

He shook his head. He would not think of her tonight. Tonight he had a willing woman who wanted him in her bed. Who spread her legs as her eyes welcomed him to do whatever he wished with her.

For the second time that night, he fell in love.

"Here." She held out her hand, then stroked it down his cock, sheathing him in a layer of something so thin and translucent, it was like it wasn't there at all. An ingenious device to catch his seed, when he spilled it.

He rubbed the head of his cock against her most sensitive parts. So wet and ready for him.

"I need to feel you inside me," she moaned, lifting her hips to grind against him.

By all the gods…he was a man, not a saint.

Odin thrust deep. Gods, she was tight around him. Was she a maiden still? Well, not now, but before he'd entered her? Dare he continue, or should he wait for her to grow accustomed to his girth?

"Yes, more, please!" she ordered.

Odin surrendered to her pleasure, for the gods knew, he wanted her just as much as she desired him.

SIX

The first orgasm rolled through Freyja like a breaking wave, and she was embarrassed to admit she squeezed his arse for every moment of it, it was so good. The second followed the first so quickly, it took her by surprise, stealing her vision for a few precious seconds so that she could do nothing but feel the incredible sensations of this man pounding away inside her.

And the third…oh, the third. She knew she was close when he suddenly stilled inside her, and she feared that in reaching his own release, he'd give her no more tonight. But while he still filled her, buried to the hilt in her core, his fingers reached for her clit and sent her spiralling into her own climax, clenching down so hard on him she feared she'd hurt him.

But he just wrapped his arms around her, pulling her against his perfectly sculpted chest, while she tried to catch her breath.

Maybe Kendall had been right. All she'd needed was some hot, hard Norse cock to help point the way to what she wanted.

Yes, she'd worked hard to be as successful in her medical career as the rest of her family, until one terrible mistake had derailed it and sent her here. But she could still be happy and successful in other ways. Maybe not as a doctor in a hospital, like she'd originally hoped, but the iceman was a new opportunity to change her life, to forge a new career out here, using all she'd learned in med school as well as the postgraduate forensic science degree she'd picked up since starting her job here.

Tomorrow, she'd draft up a press release to send to the university PR department about the find, perhaps even with some pictures, when he'd defrosted enough.

Pictures. Kendall had wanted pictures.

She glanced down. The hot Norseman's cock was still buried inside her, hot and hard like he was ready to go again. Maybe even all night.

His cock was all hers. Kendall couldn't have him. Not even a picture.

She bucked her hips against him. "Do you want some more?"

"Fuck yes," he said.

SEVEN

When she fell asleep in his arms, so sated with pleasure she still wore a smile on her face, even in sleep, Odin finally withdrew from her delicious body. Never in his life had he known such a glorious night. Even the pleasures of Valhalla would be a poor shadow in comparison.

But right now, she needed sleep, and he did not. No, what he needed to do was protect her.

Like he'd failed to do with Frigg…

Odin shook his head. He'd failed once, but he would not fail again.

Things were already different this time. For a start, the amazing sex. Not a drunken fumble in the dark that he barely remembered, over before it had really begun. No, tonight had been a feast for the senses. The sort he wished could go on for days and nights.

If only they did not need to sleep.

So while she slept, he would protect her. Learn the lay of her strange longhouse, which he'd barely glimpsed as he carried her inside. Find out if she had food supplies sufficient for the winter, and hunt for what she needed. And return to warm her bed when she awoke…

Yes. It was time to forget the past, and embrace what the fates had granted him.

Maybe even know happiness.

But only if he could protect her properly, he told himself as he slid out of her bed.

Duty before pleasure, always.

EIGHT

Freyja wasn't sure whether to be disappointed or relieved that last night's lover had left when she woke. She wouldn't have said no to another round – fuck, he'd been amazing in bed – but she'd never brought a man home or slept in the same bed as one she'd have to share breakfast with the next morning.

But if he was gone, there was nothing she could do about it. She hadn't even gotten his name or number. If she was desperate, there was definitely DNA on the condoms, but that would be a bit weird, surely. It wasn't like having a one night stand was a crime or anything.

It wasn't until she reached the kitchen that she noticed the time. Past lunchtime! She really had been up late last night, to sleep right through until afternoon. Which then begged the question…seeing as it wasn't morning any more, would it be wrong to cook one of the frozen pizzas for breakfast? It was kind of a late lunch, after all…

She dug out a Hawaiian pizza, which looked like it had been sitting in the freezer since last year's expedition, it was so covered in ice, and stuck it in the oven. She had yet to meet anyone else, back home or here in Norway, who could properly appreciate the sheer genius of putting pineapple on pizza. The salty-sweet combination, when done right, made the best pizza known to humankind. Hell, she'd happily introduce aliens to it, if they came to visit.

While the pizza was cooking, she made herself a coffee and jotted down some notes for the media release she intended to draft today.

The body had been found at the same site as that tunic Nik Fridolfsen found last year. This time, it was one of the Harald Medal winners who'd made the discovery. She thought Karl had said her name was Lauren, but it had been hard to make out. She'd have to look that up. He'd said something about a Viking weapon they'd found, too, which might have belonged to the ice mummy. Then finish up with some sort of statement wondering what stories the mummy might tell if he could talk, but with all the fancy equipment here in the lab, maybe he'll still be able to yield some interesting stories about his life and death, a thousand years ago.

She still had a few minutes, so she brought her laptop back to the cafeteria and started writing while she ate her pizza. By the time she was done – including adding Jorunn's name to the article, not Lauren — the last couple of pizza slices were as cold as the snow outside, so she stuck them in the microwave to reheat while the emailed her press release to the department's PR officer, back at the main campus.

Freyja wasn't the only one working on the weekend — Ingrid emailed back, saying she'd forwarded the press release to all the local media companies, and she'd come up on Monday with one of the university photographers to take some pictures. Oh, and the police would be coming, too. Nothing to worry about — just standard procedure when a human body was found.

Would that be convenient?

Freyja's heart sank into her slippers. The last time she'd had to talk to police about a body, she'd become the headline in the following day's newspaper. This time…

Freyja swallowed. Maybe having pizza for breakfast hadn't been the best idea after all.

No, she swore to herself. This time would

be different. This body was supposed to be here. The discovery of the century, Karl had said, and she'd believed him. Nothing would go wrong this time.

She'd run standard scans on Monday morning, and by the time the police arrived, she'd have concrete evidence to prove she hadn't been anywhere near the man when he died. Hadn't even been born.

Karl said the mummy was a Viking, and his hunches were usually right. He'd hired her to do his forensic work, despite knowing all about her background. In fact, he'd hired her because of it. So if he trusted her with his greatest discovery…she trusted him to know what he'd discovered.

Something the police couldn't possibly arrest her for.

Because this body was exactly where it was supposed to be right now, and nothing untoward was going to happen to it.

NINE

Odin had never seen a longhouse like it. Everything was made of stone and metal, with hardly any wood and no straw to be seen. Not even on the floors!

No signs of life, either. No livestock and only two people – himself, and the lady who'd taken him to her bed last night. A lady who had no servants, no thralls…yet she commanded a hall so huge it would have awed even Jarl Erik.

She had no need for him to hunt, for she had cold storage rooms filled with foodstuffs that ranged from jars full of fish through to rare delicacies he'd never heard of. Enough to feed an army.

She owned more clothing than most people wore in a year, folded into a chest on wheels, yet there was an entire store room filled with more – most of it made to fit men of his size. Though he did not feel the cold, after whatever spells Erik's witch had worked on him, it was unseemly to wander around without clothing, so he took one of the stoutly woven tunics from the store room, only to discover that the tunic had been sewn to a pair of equally stout trousers.

He had to climb into the whole ensemble from the waist, but it fit surprisingly well – like it had been made for a man of his stature. A man named OLAF, or who served someone by that name, if the letters on the breast of the strange tunic were to be believed.

There were countless boots, too, made of a substance he took for thick, hardened leather, but he had never seen a hide like this before — all fastened together in one piece, with no stitching. It beggared belief, even as he held one in his hand. Stranger still, they were made to the shape of his right foot and his left, so they fitted perfectly when he put them on.

She had no need for food or hides, and water flowed from spouts throughout the building, in a most miraculous manner. He'd heard tales of such things happening in cities far to the south, but to see it here, with his own eyes...this land he'd awoken in was wondrous indeed.

His lady had supplies enough to last her through this winter, and the next, but there was one thing she lacked: a man to protect her, and her property.

Despite his failures in the past, protection he could provide.

Except in all her wealth, something else was lacking: weapons. In all the chambers in her huge longhouse, he could not find so much as an axe for chopping wood, or a spear for catching fish. Most strange. Unless the warriors she intended to clothe and feed brought their own weapons with them…

Odin shook his head as he continued his survey of her domain.

She had several large stillrooms, with metal tables and shelves full of glass bottles filled with liquids he could not identify, even when he read the labels. Not a leaf or a blossom in sight, either, which was strange, though it might be because it was winter. He was no alewife or healer, so he could not be sure.

Tucked between the stillrooms was a scriptorium, with shelves of books, but no scribe. One book lay on the vacant desk. The words on the cover read:

ICELAB MAINTENANCE MANUAL

Odin picked it up and thumbed through the pages. The words were far less ornate than the books he'd seen before, and much easier to read as a result. There were pictures, too, but these appeared to be sketches of real things within the building, like the box on the wall with the mysteriously blinking red light. Apparently, if he pressed several of the buttons, the box would be armed.

Was this why he'd found no weapons? Were the boxes weapons? Perhaps magically firing arrows or poison or releasing a plague of vipers or...

No, he would not play with things he did not yet understand. First, he would complete his survey of her domain. Then, he would read the book. Then, when he knew all he could know about this place, then he would arm what defences she had, so that he might better protect her.

At last, he came to a door with a warning sign that read:

CAUTION: OUTER DOOR CAN BE BLOCKED BY SNOW. PLEASE USE SHOVEL PROVIDED.

Finally – something Odin understood. He could shovel snow with the best of them. One particularly bad winter, the snow had piled up around the longhouse as high as the roof, and they'd had to dig their way out. He, Thor and Loki had turned it into a contest, to see who could clear a path to the outbuildings first. He'd won, of course, with Thor not far behind. Loki hadn't even reached the yardhouse when Thor stepped in to help him. For the first time, he wondered where they were, and why they were not here with him. Jarl Erik's witch had enchanted both of them before his eyes, while Erik promised they would rise at his command when the time came.

Yet none of them were here now. A mystery to solve for another day. Right now, he had to dig his lady's longhouse out of the snow, before the new storm he could see coming buried it any deeper.

Odin pushed open the door, shouldering his shovel, and stepped into watery sunlight.

And turned to stone.

TEN

If the police were paying her a visit, then she should probably make sure she hadn't left university property along the side of the road to be damaged or stolen, Freyja told herself as she rugged up to go retrieve the scooter.

One look out the front door had her swearing and headed back to the supply room to borrow a pair of snow boots. She hadn't bothered to bring her own with her because it was supposed to be the height of summer, with record ice melt due to global warming — hardly the time to have a snowstorm.

Yet here she was, trudging through snow in her borrowed boots, determined to find and bring back that scooter before those thunderheads coming over the mountains arrived. She hadn't checked the weather forecast, but she didn't need to know the specifics to be sure those clouds looked bad.

When she reached the road, she wouldn't have found the scooter if it weren't for a wheel sticking up from the snowdrift on the opposite side of the road to the one she'd flown into. Worse, the snow around it had hardened to ice overnight, so it was a bastard of a job to dig the bloody thing out. Twice, she'd considered going back to the lab for a shovel, but she wasn't sure it would be much use against the ice.

Eventually, she managed to drag the ice covered contraption onto the road, where she kicked enough frost from the tyres to get them to move, so she could slowly wheel it back up the driveway.

Her arms felt ready to fall off by the time she reached the end of the driveway, and turned the scooter around the corner of the building, toward the garage.

Only to find the snow was too deep to go any further. While she'd been busy with her hot Norseman last night, it must have snowed again, and all of it had been blown into the courtyard, burying the helipad, the ugly sundial, and any chance she had of leaving the lab via any mode of transport other than her own booted feet.

God, and it was getting dark, with no sunlight to be seen. The clouds that had been hanging over the mountains earlier were looming over the lab now, and snowflakes were already falling. The wind had started to pick up, but they were in the lee of the building here, so the wind hadn't reached the courtyard yet. So when she saw movement…

She wanted to thank every god that had ever

existed. So there was a maintenance man, after all. She'd never been so thankful to see a man with a shovel in all her life.

"Hey, you! Any chance you can help me clear a path to the garage, so I can put this away before the storm hits?" she shouted.

He turned.

The scooter would have dropped from her suddenly nerveless hands if the front wheel weren't firmly stuck in a snowdrift.

It was HIM. The owner of that hot Norse cock she'd ridden half the night. Only now he was wearing overalls and instead of those firm hands wrapped around every curve of her naked body, he was holding a shovel.

She'd fucked the maintenance man?

The incredibly hot, muscled beast of a maintenance man.

Had he been wearing an eyepatch last night, or had she been too intent on the rest of him to even notice that particular detail?

She shook her head. It had been a one night stand, a night of meaningless sex where they hadn't bothered to exchange numbers or even names. It meant nothing. Sure, one look at him and she could feel him thrusting hard between her thighs, but she could ignore that.

What mattered was that she was in charge here at the lab, and he was just the maintenance man. He was here to do his job, so she could do hers.

Which meant she had to be professional, and in control, and pretend her underwear wasn't totally soaked at the sight of him. She fixed her gaze on his chest. On the name badge on his chest. Not thinking of any of the hard muscles underneath the overalls at all. AT ALL.

"Olaf, right? You're the maintenance man here? Shovelling snow?" she asked.

She was pretty sure he'd spoken English last night, but now she wasn't certain. Her Norwegian was limited, so if he didn't, this was going to be a whole lot harder than it had to be.

Or not hard enough, her traitorous libido

sniggered.

Even the clouds were trying to help her, sending a flurry of flakes between them so she couldn't see him for a moment.

"Ja, I shovel snow for you," he said, in that same deep voice that seemed to make things vibrate deep in her core.

"Can you clear a path to that shed so I can put this away?" she asked, pointing.

"I can, but there is an easier way," he said, striding through the snow as easily as if it was air. He lifted the scooter onto his shoulder, then turned and walked toward the shed. Like the bloody thing weighed nothing.

She couldn't help it. She just stood and stared. Sure, the overalls hid a lot, but nothing could hide the bulge of his muscles as he carried an entire scooter across the courtyard, and into the garage. When he emerged, she was still standing there, feeling stupid.

"Would you like me to carry you inside again, too?" he asked.

Fuck yes. And hell no.

If he lifted her in his arms again, she was totally going to take him to bed, not caring that she was his boss and that she'd be in a whole lot of trouble if anyone found out and…

Fuck he was hot. She was surprised the snow wasn't steaming around his feet.

"I'll be fine," she said airily, turning away so she could head toward the front door. The snow was falling harder now, turning the drive from black to white. Even the steps were dusted with snow, and those clouds were darker than night, even if it was still midafternoon.

She knocked the snow off her boots, then walked in her socks down the corridor past the labs to the loading dock, where the outdoor gear was supposed to be kept.

She could hear the scrape of his shovel against the snow outside the loading dock door.

He should come inside, instead of staying out there in this storm. There was no point shovelling snow if it was only going to come down harder as the storm worsened.

He'd saved her last night, but as his boss, she was supposed to be responsible for his safety. She should open the door and tell him to come inside.

She was not going to do anything inappropriate when he came in. She could control herself.

Freyja punched the button to open the loading dock door.

Wind howled into the building, showering her in snow. She coughed and spluttered for a moment, before she cupped her hands to her mouth and shouted, "You need to come inside, out of the storm. It's not safe out there!"

A rumbling laugh came out of the darkness. "I will be fine. I will come inside when I am finished."

Sleeping with one of her staff was bad enough, but letting him get injured because of her own silliness was way worse. He'd only been wearing overalls. Not even proper snow gear. If he stayed out there much longer, he might freeze to death.

And that would be a terrible loss to the world. Even if she could never share a bed with him again.

"I must insist. The university safety procedures state that everyone has to take shelter inside during a snowstorm. They even extended the accommodation block so that a whole expedition team could stay here in case of bad weather." Oh god. He'd have to sleep here another night. She wasn't going to sleep a wink. "I must insist you come inside."

"I am almost finished. Once I am done, then I shall come inside, and not before."

The shovel scraped again, but she couldn't see him amid the whirling snow outside. It looked like a freaking blizzard out there. What kind of lunatic insisted on shovelling snow in a blizzard?

"Get inside now!" she ordered, with the voice of a Doctor Dealing With Life or Death.

"Miss…"

"It's Freyja. Doctor Freyja Valdis, actually, but as we tend to keep things pretty informal at the university, Freyja will be fine."

He appeared at the door, looming larger than she remembered. His eye gleamed blue like the summer sky should have been, as he dusted snow out of his golden hair. "As you command, Doctor Freyja, I am coming inside with you now." He grinned, as if he knew exactly how his words sounded.

And then his grin disappeared, as all the lights went out.

"Fuck!' she said, spitting out another mouthful of snow. She needed to get the door shut, and that wasn't happening without electricity. "Go get the power back on, and then come right back so I can close this door!"

ELEVEN

Odin nodded, and turned back to the storm. He had no idea how to do what she'd ordered him to do, but she'd pointed up at the roof, and he vaguely remembered a picture in the manual showing a ladder to the roof, which he could just make out through the swirling snow. What he'd do once he reached the roof, he wasn't sure, but if that's what she wanted…he shrugged and headed up.

Snow had piled up on the roof as well, which was topped by strange black glass tiles, each one as big as a bed. The tiles were pitched at a sharp enough angle that the snow slid right off, but it was coming down thick and fast now, so it was only a matter of time before the piles rose high enough to topple over onto the tiles, and cover those as well.

An angry squawk made him peer under the nearest tile…and almost lose his good eye to a well-aimed beak.

Odin backed away from the raven and its nest. No, two ravens…with nestlings beneath them. He'd always had a soft spot for ravens, so he took a moment to shape the snow into a barrier that blocked the nest from the worst of the storm. "I'll bring you some food later. The gods know we have enough to spare," he promised the birds.

He scanned the roof again. There was no sign of any threat, or anything else he could do, so he grabbed the side rails of the ladder and began to descend.

"Good work! The lights are back on, so get in here now and help me shut this door!" he heard her say faintly over the wind.

Odin grinned and obeyed.

TWELVE

She did her best to avoid him for the rest of the evening. When he entered the cafeteria, she grabbed her things and left, making sure to keep her bedroom door closed so she definitely didn't know which of the guest rooms he'd chosen, which meant she couldn't possibly knock on his door in the middle of the night, no matter how tempting that might be.

She even went to bed early, in the hope that she could fall asleep and not think about him for a few hours, but sleep refused to come.

Instead, all she could think about was the previous night. How amazing he'd looked naked. How his hot hard length had driven her to undreamt-of peaks of pleasure and how she'd wanted to do it all again when she woke up this morning. No, afternoon.

The one-eyed monster of a maintenance man. No, his eye, not his monstrous…

Fuck. She'd never been this needy in her life, but if there was one thing she knew well, it was anatomy, so she pleasured herself as best she could (trying not to think about how much better it would be if it were his huge hands doing this and not her own) before she finally dropped off to sleep.

Only to wake in the dark, absolutely fucking freezing. She reached for the light, but that wasn't working either.

She swore. The power had gone out again. Which meant she had to do the one thing she'd sworn she wouldn't – go and tell Olaf the maintenance man that she needed him.

She fumbled for the torch she'd left on her bedside table, as insurance against another blackout.

It had to be Olaf's fault, she fumed as she pulled on a coat over her pyjamas. He hadn't fixed the power properly, which was why it had gone out again.

She headed up the corridor, checking every guest room, before sweeping her torch beam around the bunkroom. No Olaf.

Maybe she'd underestimated him, and he was already working on the problem.

Freyja found him in the cafeteria, reading a book. Under cafeteria lights that worked just fine.

She blew out a frustrated breath that no longer misted the air. The heating was working in here, too. It wasn't all that warm, but it was better than nothing.

"The power's out in the accommodation block. Can you fix it?" she asked.

He glanced up. "I am not sure. I am not familiar with these…electrical systems. I am trying to learn about them. Do you know much about this back up system?"

The hospitals back home had backup generators, to keep the power on in a blackout. Only the backup generator didn't power the entire building, just the essential systems, including life support, which was why you had to check what you plugged the machines into, to make sure the socket was connected to the backup system. If things worked the same way here…

"Backup systems are usually only connected to the most essential things," she said slowly. But what were the most essential things here? Keeping the artefacts safe, or stopping the staff from freezing to death? A little bit of cold air wouldn't hurt the artefacts, which had all survived centuries buried in ice, but humans were a whole lot more fragile. Surely the university hadn't… "Let me see that," she ordered, grabbing the book from Olaf.

She flipped to the pages on the backup system. Luckily, this was the English manual and not the Norwegian one, so she could mostly make sense of it. Essential systems were…oh. Everything in the main lab building, but not the accommodation annexe. So the cafeteria had heat, light and an operational kitchen, and the ice mummy in the basement got to continue defrosting at a nice, constant temperature, but unless she wanted to freeze to death like he had, she'd have to find somewhere else to sleep. In a lab or the cafeteria or…the library.

The labs were out because the doors all had electronic locks, which might not be working properly after the power outage, and no way did she want to get trapped in one of those, without food or a bathroom.

The cafeteria could work, for there was plenty of space, easy access to food and water, with bathrooms right outside. The only problem was that she'd have to wrestle a mattress up two flights of narrow stairs before she could sleep there, and her arms still ached from dragging the scooter back.

But the library was on the same level as the guest rooms, plus it was a whole lot more private than the cafeteria…

He might not be responsible for her frigid room, but he could have at least warned her that it might happen when he'd turned the backup system on. So it was still partially his problem, and he could bloody well help her fix it, at least for tonight.

She handed the book back to Olaf. "It looks like we're on backup power, which only works in this part of the building. Until mains power is restored, we'll have to sleep here in the lab building instead of the guest rooms. Can you help me drag a mattress into the library?"

He set the book down on the table. "Of course."

It took two of them to wrestle her mattress down the narrow corridors and into the library, which got its name from the shelves lining one wall, filled with a mixture of academic texts and tattered novels. She let go, and the mattress thumped to the floor, taking up most of the available space.

"I will help you carry the bedding," Olaf said, leaving.

It wasn't until she'd finished making up the bed, with pillows and linen and a couple of extra blankets she'd found in the cupboard that she realised there was no space for another mattress for Olaf.

Who had already begun stripping out of his overalls.

Holy fuck.

She'd noticed his muscles before, but now she looked at him, really looked at him…

She needed to keep her hands off him. Even if they had to share a bed and he was going to be doing it…

Gulp.

Naked.

"No funny business. Keep your hands to yourself," she said. "We're only sharing a bed to keep warm. That's it. Hopefully the power will be back on tomorrow and we can go back to normal sleeping arrangements."

Olaf nodded. "As you wish."

Well if he could sound that professional and disinterested…like last night's sex had been nothing out of the ordinary for him…so could she.

"Good night," she said, climbing under the covers and turning her back to him. If she didn't look, then she wouldn't be tempted to do something she shouldn't.

"Sleep well, Doctor Freyja," he replied, as he slid in beside her.

At first, she couldn't sleep, hearing his every breath and wondering if he was going to say something. Or do something.

The next thing she knew, she was pressed against something hot and hard and her hands were wrapped around...

Fuck. She rolled over, put her back to him, and stuck her hands firmly under her pillow, glad he couldn't see her blush burning in the dark.

An hour later, she woke up again. This time, she'd hooked her leg over his and was all but dry humping him.

She jerked away.

"Doctor Freyja, is there something you wish to ask me?" his voice rumbled out of the darkness.

Fuck. She had woken him up.

"No. Just…we're only sharing a bed to keep each other warm, right? Nothing else."

She heard him shift, then felt the mattress move as he rose. Then the door opened and closed, and he was gone.

She let out a long breath she hadn't known she was holding. Fuck. Fuck. Fuck.

THIRTEEN

He could sleep beside a woman, even snuggle up to her for warmth, and not put a finger past propriety. He'd done it for years with Frigg, who he knew had no wish for his body in any romantic sense. But Freyja, whose hands caressed and stroked, who'd even pressed her wet centre against him as she'd started to climb on top of him…now she was driving him well into the realms of madness, for she obviously wanted him as much as he wanted her.

That's when he remembered the little sheaths from last night – the ones she'd said would keep them safe from little surprises. He'd seen a box of them in one of the store rooms during his explorations earlier, so he left to get some.

Her breathing was still rapid and uneven when he opened the door to the scriptorium, so he knew she wasn't asleep. He tossed the square packages onto the bed. All except for one, which he opened so he might sheath himself with the sticky casing inside.

Then he lay beside her on the bed, ready for her.

"Doctor Freyja, you may safely mount me now," he said, when she did not immediately do so.

"I can what?"

"You were trying to climb on top of me before. I am now wearing one of your condoms and I am ready for you. To keep you warm, like you want."

"I don't..." she spluttered.

"Doctor Freyja, you are wet for me, just like last night. I am just as ready for you. For all the fucking you want." He reached for her hand, and wrapped it around his sheathed cock. He half expected her to yank her hand away, as she had before, but this time, she did not.

"You really are...huge, aren't you?"

Odin smiled in the dark. "But you can take me."

She squirmed beneath the blankets beside him. Taking off her clothing? He hoped so.

A moment later, she — and the blankets — shifted to cover him. "This is just to keep warm," he heard her say.

Then she eased herself down upon his length and began to ride him. Tentatively at first, then harder and faster, so he took hold of her hips and matched her thrust for thrust, until she was gasping, moaning, then screaming his name (or the name she'd called him — he still hadn't bothered to correct her), not once, but over and over, until he thought she was spent.

"Are you warm enough now?" he asked, ready to help her lie down beside him.

"I want…more…" she said.

So he flipped her over instead, covering her body with his, but he didn't enter her again just yet.

"Tell me you want me," he said.

Frigg would never have said the words. But Freyja…she hesitated.

"We're just keeping warm," she said weakly.

He pressed the tip of his cock against her folds, rubbing that sensitive spot so she gasped.

"Tell me what you want," he said.

He knew what he wanted – to fuck her all night, and protect her every other moment he wasn't in her bed. But this was about her.

She swallowed. "I want you to fuck me. Hot and hard like last night."

He tried to take it slow, but the glorious tightness as she closed around him drove him wild. He pounded into her, as she cried and begged for more, until he roared her name at the peak of his own pleasure, then fucked her some more.

FOURTEEN

When Freyja's breathing slowed into sleep, he carefully withdrew and went outside to check on the storm. The blizzard still raged, so he headed back inside, hoping that by reading the maintenance manual, he might learn enough about this building to keep her warm without a fire.

For he could not fuck her every moment of the day and night, no matter how much he wanted to.

It was nearly morning, too. He should take his book for a walk around the building, matching the sections to the equipment they explained, until he actually understood it all.

Freyja would forgive him for not warming her all night, if he found a way to warm the whole building once more, he was sure of it.

And he needed to take the ravens some food, before he forgot, too, and hope they survived the blizzard. He'd promised, after all.

FIFTEEN

The second morning…no, afternoon…in a row, Freyja woke up alone. This time, she was definitely aching for him. She'd never liked rough sex before, but with him…he could pound her all night, and she'd still beg for more. Or climb on top of him and ride him…

God, she could barely believe she'd done that last night. He was her subordinate, for fuck's sake. A sexual harassment case just waiting to happen.

Unless they could just forget about it, and pretend it hadn't happened.

After all, the first night hadn't meant anything to him, so the second probably hadn't, either. The power would be back on by now, so they wouldn't have to share a room again, let alone a bed, or huddle together for warmth.

She shook herself. The last thing she should be thinking about right now was hot sex, especially after she'd had so much of it. What she should be doing was taking a look at how well the body in the necropsy fridge was defrosting, to see whether she could at least x-ray it before the police arrived tomorrow. Because everything would go so much more smoothly tomorrow if she could confidently say Karl and Jorunn had found a Viking, instead of some modern day murder victim.

Well, they still might have been murdered, just…far enough in the past that the killer was likely to be just as dead as their victim.

Just as long as the police left without arresting her. Was that too much to ask?

She'd also like it if they kept her name out of the news, but if this body really was the find of the century, like Karl said, because Otzi the iceman was so last century, news headlines were probably inevitable. And if her name was in the news for a good reason, linked with an incredible discovery…that could only be a good thing, right?

She stopped off in her (still freezing) guest room to get her camera, so she could get some good preliminary shots of the ice mummy. The university had several of them in the supply room and one mounted on a set of scaffolding up on the ceiling of the scanner room, but she always felt more comfortable with her own equipment.

Besides, if any of the pictures from the university cameras got wiped because of the power outage, at least she'd have the ones she'd taken. She knew Karl took backups when he was out at site for the same reason. They'd even taken extra solar panels to charge all the equipment this trip. Freyja shook her head. She'd never get used to the idea of solar panels in the snow. Or snow at all, really.

Thinking about snow…how bad was the blizzard last night? Surely it had stopped snowing by now.

Freyja peeked through the glass front door, and was surprised to see…nothing, really. Everything was white.

Usually, you could see the curve of the driveway, and the road in the distance, with the village up on the next hill, but she might as well have been in Antarctica for all she could see now. There was snow piled up as high as the steps, with a drift even covering most of the doormat. And there were snowflakes still floating down from a sky that was almost as dark as yesterday, when she'd ordered Olaf inside.

She hoped he wasn't out there shovelling snow again. They'd need earthmoving equipment to shift this load, or a week of proper summer weather, because one man's muscles and a shovel just wouldn't cut it.

But she wasn't supposed to be thinking about Olaf right now. All of her focus should be on the ice mummy, and what she might discover.

She forced herself to head for the necropsy lab, no matter how much she wanted a coffee, because she'd learned the hard way that it was best to deal with dead bodies before breakfast.

She scanned her security card at the door and breathed a sigh of relief that the electronic locks were still working. Not that anyone would want to break into this lab to steal stuff, but there were valuable artefacts in the climate-controlled artefact rooms, like coins and jewellery and things, which would probably fetch a high price on the illegal antiquities market. Or so she imagined, seeing as she knew nothing about illegal markets at all, but the legal market…which seemed to be a kind of catfight between museums, as far as she could tell…were already salivating over the finds, and competing to design an exhibit worthy of displaying them. She hoped whoever got the ice mummy would be willing to show them to the world. Some discoveries needed to be shared, and not hidden away. Whoever the mummy had been in life was nothing compared to how famous they'd be in death.

If Karl was right…

Freyja reached for the door handle to the walk-in refrigerator. She took a deep breath, then prayed silently that this discovery would change her life for the better. She wasn't even sure who or what she directed the prayer to, as she wasn't the least bit religious. Maybe the Judeo-Christian god, or the Norse pantheon the mummy had believed in. Who had the leader of the Norse gods been again?

She considered reaching for her phone to check, before she remembered – it was Odin, the one they called the All-Father. Not because he screwed anything that moved like Zeus, but because he was considered the guy responsible for creation, or so Lara had told her one night at the end of last season, after a lot of aquavit.

"Odin, I could do with a bit of your favour right now," she said as she yanked down the handle, and threw the door open.

"Fuck me," she breathed at what she saw.

The autopsy table sat in the middle of the fridge, just where she'd left it, awash with water, but the body was gone.

"Odin, you are an arsehole," she snapped, as she slammed the door.

SIXTEEN

Freyja could see the headlines already. It'd be THE BODY THIEF STRIKES AGAIN everywhere from here to home, never mind that she'd never stolen a single body, let alone this one. The media hadn't cared about destroying her life and livelihood last time – all they'd cared about was getting more traffic to their websites with their horrible clickbait headlines, and this time would be no different.

And with the police coming tomorrow…they'd arrest her for sure.

Even worse was how devastated Karl would be, having finally found his holy grail…only for it to go missing. Getting arrested would almost be a relief if it meant she wouldn't see Karl's face when he found out the body was missing.

Unless she could find the body before the police arrived.

If she could, then no one need ever know it had gone missing.

Only it could be anywhere by now. If someone had stolen it while she'd been on that video call to her family, before her attempt to pick up at the pub, they could be anywhere within a two day drive. They could be anywhere in Europe by now…if they hadn't put the body on a plane, in which case it could be absolutely anywhere.

Except…she hadn't seen tyre tracks in the snow when she'd taken the scooter out, which was why she hadn't seen the ice patch until she hit it. Nor had there been any tyre tracks when she'd wheeled the scooter back from the crash site yesterday, and then the blizzard had hit, and no one with any sense would have been out in that.

Even now, the roads were impassable, and there was no way a helicopter could have landed in the courtyard without her noticing.

Which meant the body had to still be on the premises. Hidden somewhere.

Either in cold storage, or in a box big enough to keep it cool until they could transport it to a buyer. She couldn't miss something that big, and whoever had hidden it had likely used a trolley to take it to its hiding place, so she could probably limit her search to anywhere you could take a trolley. But not the mortuary trolley, because they'd left that in the fridge.

Which was weird, really. Why wouldn't you take the trolley it was already on?

Unless the new trolley was the way they intended to transport it offsite, when the roads were clear.

So she was probably looking for something big, with wheels.

After all, it wasn't like the body had gotten up and hidden itself. That thing had been dead for at least a thousand years.

Mummies didn't move except in really weird movies, and she definitely wasn't in one of those. She was far too practical for that sort of thing.

She marched out to start her search.

SEVENTEEN

It wasn't until Freyja was finished checking the fridges and freezers in the kitchen that she realised she hadn't actually had breakfast yet. So while she waited for another frozen pizza to cook, she paced across the cafeteria, trying to work out where she hadn't looked yet.

Because wherever it was, that's where the body had to be.

As she chewed thoughtfully on a slice of

pizza, she mused on where she'd hide a body, if she really was a body thief.

Somewhere it wouldn't be found, obviously. Somewhere no one else would go.

Well, no one would be crazy enough to go outside in this weather, that was for sure. But if they'd stolen the body as soon as it had arrived, before the storm started…maybe…

Swearing, she headed down to the loading dock, where she'd left her snow gear. Crossing the snow filled courtyard provoked even more swearing, but she had to be sure. One by one, she trudged to each of the outbuildings, and checked those. One shed held the waste barrels, which she left well alone. The body was too big to fit in one of those, unless someone cut it up, and what was the point of that? The ice mummy was important because it was intact.

Unless it really was a modern murder victim…

No. No one went out to the Jotunheimen Mountains for anything except hiking or an archaeological dig, and if someone had gone missing out there, she'd have seen something about it.

This was Karl's ice mummy. The body wouldn't be in a barrel.

Gardening tools, hazardous chemicals, more shovels, a whole lot of salt and something that looked like a cross between a lawn mower and a mulching machine, which she figured must be a snow blower or something, seeing as it had SNO written on the side.

Just like inside the main building, there were no bodies here, either. Not that she really expected there to be. She'd struggled to reach the other side of the courtyard, just by herself. Carrying something huge like a corpse…no, it just wasn't possible.

Her traitorous memory popped up an image of Olaf, his muscles bulging through his overalls as he lifted the scooter like it was weightless, striding through the snow with effortless ease.

He could have done it. Not just on Friday,

but any time since the helicopter had landed. After all, she'd slept late yesterday and today, and who else was here but the two of them? They were snowed in, for Odin's sake. If she wasn't the body thief, then he had to be.

Now, if she was a massive Norse muscle man who wanted to steal the body of one of his ancestors, where would she put it? Somewhere she'd never look, and never reach, but also where it would be easy to transport.

Had he taken the scooter to the garage not just to be nice, but to keep her from finding the body?

If he had, she was going to kick him in that massive groin of his. It was a big enough target.

She marched to the garage and kicked at the door until the ice freezing it shut fell away, then threw the door open. It was half full of cars, most belonging to the expedition crew, all with the keys inside, in case anyone needed to move them while the owners were out at the site.

A quick scan of the garage told her the body wasn't in sight, so she tried the cars next. Opening all the doors and the boot of each one, only to come up empty.

Damn it, where was it? She would have put it in the back of a car, for easy transport. The garage was easily as cold as the mortuary fridge, so it wasn't like keeping it cold would be an issue. It could stay out here until the snow melted…if it was here. Which it wasn't.

Which left…where?

She stomped outside, slamming the garage door behind her. She'd looked everywhere. Tramped all over snow that shouldn't be here in summer. And she still hadn't found the bloody body.

If Olaf was watching her, she'd bet he was laughing his arse off. She could almost imagine him standing there in the courtyard, snow shovel in hand, massive muscled shoulders shaking as he hid his mirth behind one huge hand.

Fuck, was that really the answer? So fucking

simple she hadn't even thought of it?

Because why would any sane person go out in a snowstorm…unless they were burying a body in the snow?

Freyja seized a shovel and began to dig.

EIGHTEEN

Odin waited until it was dark enough to venture outside before heading up to the roof to check on the ravens. The snowfall had faded to just a few flakes at a time, and he was surprised to find the ravens – parents and babies – had weathered the storm quite well, and while they were initially hostile, they soon calmed down when he laid out the table scraps from Freyja's last meal.

He did notice that the black tiles were now covered with snow, which the maintenance manual said was not a good thing. He wanted to ask Freyja's advice on the correct course of action first, though, for she was surely more familiar with these magical power systems than he was. All the knowledge he had came from a few pictures in a book.

The temperature was definitely dropping, with more snow on the way, so he should find her sooner rather than later to make sure the work was finished before the next wave of this storm hit.

He was just about to descend into the building again to search for Freyja, when he noticed movement on the ground.

What in the gods' name…?

He headed down to the courtyard instead. "What are you doing?"

She huffed out a breath and set down her shovel. "I'm looking for the missing body, only I haven't found it yet, which is why I'm still digging. Care to enlighten me, or are you just going to try to distract me with your dick again?"

Frigg had said and done many puzzling things in their time together, but Freyja made him feel like a witless fool.

She evidently knew it, too, for she grabbed his arm like he was a wayward toddler. "Come with me, and I'll show you." She took him to a room with metal tables, then stopped outside the door. "This is where I put the ice mummy to defrost on Friday. This is where it still should be, except it isn't." She patted her pockets, then scowled. "I left my security pass down in the loading bay. You'll have to open the door."

Obediently, Odin grabbed the handle, but it did not budge. "I do not believe I can." Unless she wanted him to break the door, which he suspected he could, but then he would have to repair it, and he did not know nearly enough about working glass or metal to do that.

She swore. "Fine, I'll go get mine. You stay right here and don't move until I get back."

She stormed off before he could mention the possible power problems.

She returned soon enough with a small palm-sized rectangle that she swiped across a box with a blinking light, which went from red to green. Now she could turn the door handle with no effort at all.

He wouldn't mind a magic card like that. "Where do I get such a card?" he asked.

She frowned. "The university issues them pretty much the day you start, because you can't access most of the staff areas without one. Out here, though…maybe yours is still in the post. I guess I could take a look in the office, in case it's already arrived, but no one thought to open it…" She shook her head. "But that's not important. What is important is what's supposed to be here and isn't!" She strode into the room, then yanked open a second door that led to a cold storage chamber. "What do you see that's wrong with this picture?" She waved at the interior, as mist curled around her boots.

Odin looked inside. "There is very little here. A lot of empty shelves, and a table on wheels with a tub full of water." He stepped inside and peered into the tub. "Just a short hunting spear." He pulled it out of the water, the weight achingly familiar in his hand.

He'd set this spear in Loki's hand, the day his family had died. He would have done the same for Vali and Vidarr, when they were old enough. But now the only hand left to hold it was his.

Freyja blinked. "I didn't see that before. It must have been frozen in the ice with the body. The one that isn't here. Do you know where it is?"

From the fury in her expression, she evidently expected him to be able to answer her. But Odin could only shake his head. "You are looking for a man's body? One that you believe should be here?"

His first thought was Loki, the most likely man to wield Odin's spear, for Thor favoured his father's hammer, unwieldy though it was.

But Loki would have only feigned death, and the moment no one was watching, shifted into a smaller, swifter creature so he could flee. Then he would return later, with information to help everyone. That was why he was the best scout they'd ever had.

"Where is it, Olaf?"

"I do not know. I had no idea you kept a corpse in here. The only things I have seen in the cold storage chambers are food supplies. Who would steal a body, yet leave such a valuable spear behind?"

She held out her hand. "Let me see that." She peered closely at the carvings, then dropped it back onto the table, beside the water filled tub. "I just know those are Viking runes. Karl or one of the others will know what it means."

Interesting. Freyja could read the maintenance manual well enough, so it had not occurred to him that she could not read this as well.

"This is a hunting blessing, invoking the

gods' favour for it to fly straight and true," Odin said, pointing at the first line of runes. "These are the names of the men who have wielded it, in a direct line from father to son." The last name was his own, carved by his father on the night he'd become a man. He'd never had a chance to decide which of his sons would wield it after him. Now he never would. "Only a fool would leave this behind." He'd left it behind, the night Frigg died. She'd fought with it to protect their sons and herself, but it had not been enough.

Freyja sighed, as if she shared his pain. "Yeah, well, we should leave it here for now, where it'll be safe. Or as safe as anything can be, with people stealing bodies." She led the way out into the corridor, and Odin followed.

The door had just clicked closed before the lights blinked out.

"Fuck. Not again," Freyja said.

Odin coughed. "Ah, I forgot. I was supposed to tell you that the backup power comes from the black solar panels on the roof, charging a battery, and the storm covered them with snow, so we will need to clear the snow off them if we want more power."

She huffed out a breath. "You have got to be the worst maintenance man I ever met."

NINETEEN

Why he couldn't have told her about the solar panels when it was still daylight, she didn't know. Or why he hadn't just gone and cleaned the bloody things himself without waiting for…what? Her permission to do his fucking job?

Even in the dark, he could evidently feel her fury. "I intended to tell you earlier, only you were digging in the snow, and then you brought me up here, as this seemed more urgent, and…" He coughed. "I am not familiar with solar panels, so I hope you can help."

She'd bloody well have to, wouldn't she? Not like she could trust Olaf to get it right.

First stealing stuff, and now this. What kind of maintenance man was he, anyway?

One who didn't have access to the necropsy lab, or the fridge, her traitorous subconscious whispered.

Which kind of meant he couldn't possibly have stolen the body. And she'd seen the way he looked at that spear. Like he'd wanted it, but he'd set it down without a backward glance.

But if he hadn't stolen the body, and she knew she hadn't…who had? And where was it?

Freyja shook her head. In the dark, facing a night with no power, she had bigger things to worry about. She could worry about the corpse in the morning when the power came back on.

She'd left her torch in the library, but she

still had her phone, and the flashlight app that would shine the way until the battery on that died, at least.

"Let's get a couple of lanterns from the supply room, and head up to the roof. The sooner we get this done, the better," she said.

At the base of the stairs to the roof, there were a bunch of brooms, all labelled FOR SOLAR PANELS ONLY.

So that was how you dealt with solar panels and snow. She grabbed two brooms and handed one to Olaf. Somehow he'd already acquired a shovel, and Freyja wasn't going to argue. She'd had enough shovelling snow today to last her for two lifetimes, at least.

Sweeping the snow off the solar panels was kind of cathartic, actually. She was still pissed off that the mummy was missing, still fuming that the power was out and the man on the roof with her was responsible for it being out until at least morning, but at least she could do something about it. Well, that wasn't hitting him with the broom. Tempting though that was, it wouldn't make anything better. She'd probably only miss him and hit one of the solar panels instead, anyway.

She finished clearing one panel, but it was a hard slog through semi-frozen snow to get to the next one, especially as it was up past her waist. But they had to clear the snow off all the panels, or there'd be no power tomorrow.

Olaf set down his broom. "You keep cleaning the panels. I will shovel snow."

"But you can't use the shovel. It'll scratch the panels," she began, then closed her mouth.

He most certainly could use the shovel, scooping up big piles of snow and sending them tumbling down to the ground below. One after the other, in an avalanche that would bury anyone unlucky enough to be standing in the courtyard. Burying all her work from this afternoon, too, if he had hidden the body out there.

Which even she was finding hard to believe. Sure, she hadn't stolen it, and he was the only other person here, but her gut told her he wasn't a body thief, either.

Or maybe that was her core, getting so excited about his cock it didn't care what else he might be capable of.

Like clearing the roof of snow, so by the time she had to head to the next panel, she could actually see the roof panels beneath her feet.

Halfway along, she was definitely flagging. She should never have tried to dig up the whole courtyard, no matter what she suspected was hidden there. But he was still going strong, not slowing in the slightest. If anything, he seemed to be moving faster, already clearing around the base of the panel three ahead of her.

She swiped at the next panel with her broom, and lost her grip on the handle. The broom went flying, sending a gobbet of snow soaring across the roof to splat against Olaf's back.

Shit. She might have fantasised about whacking him, but that had been a complete accident. She waited for him to turn around so she could apologise.

Only he didn't even seem to have noticed.

Maybe it hadn't hit him that hard, or he was just more used to the cold, being a native Norwegian and all. Or maybe he was enjoying his snow shovelling so much he hadn't even noticed.

She retrieved her broom, and swept a load of snow down to where she could reach it. Then she scooped up a double handful and began to shape it into a ball.

Yes, it was childish. No, she probably shouldn't do this. But it was better than hitting him with a broom for being so frustrating and hot all at the same time.

She drew her arm back and let fly with the snowball. It soared right over his head and smashed on the next solar panel.

Now who was useless?

He turned. "Doctor Freyja? Are you all right?"

"No. I was trying to hit you," she admitted.

He nodded. "You need to aim better." He shaped his own snowball, but instead of throwing it at her, he lobbed it into the courtyard – right at that stupid sundial, sticking out of the snow.

Of course he hit his target, which thrummed like a gong at the blow.

"I can teach you," he said.

She grabbed another handful of snow. "I don't need help throwing things!" This one skimmed his shoulder, then careened off into the darkness.

He just grinned. "Yes, you do. Would you believe I stunned a reindeer with a snowball once? I hit it right between the eyes, and it just keeled over, right in front of me on the snow. When it woke up, I taught it to pull my sled."

"That is complete bullshit, I bet," she declared.

Olaf held up both hands. "It is the truth, I swear."

She considered for a moment. She knew there were reindeer herders in the mountains, and she'd analysed enough dead reindeer for Karl and his team here in the lab. If Olaf was from around here, maybe even living with the herders, he might not be lying. "I suppose you called it Rudolph, then," she said, setting her hands on her hips.

"No, I called her Dvoran. It means sleep," he said.

This time, she actually believed him. He might not be much of a maintenance man, but he was a champion snow-shoveler and a reindeer trainer.

"I've never seen a real, live reindeer. Only pictures of them, and the remains that come in from the mountains," she admitted.

"Well, it is no wonder if you cannot hit your target. You will frighten them away," Olaf said. He went back to shovelling.

Reluctantly, she retrieved her broom and went to work on the next panel. After a moment, she said, "You know, there aren't any reindeer where I'm from. No snow, either."

"Then what are you doing so far from

home?"

"You mean, when I'm not clearing snow and searching for missing bodies?" She considered for a moment. "Maybe running away from my failures, or at least the people who remind me of them, all the time. What I could have had, if things hadn't gone so wrong. Working out what I can have, now all that I wanted is gone." Before she could say anything else, she went back to work, scrubbing fiercely at the panel surface to get the ice off.

"Then you are very brave, to come so far and try new things, when you have lost so much."

She blinked. Now he was complimenting her? "I'm not brave. I'm a coward, running from things instead of facing them. Not that there's anything left to face any more, even if I wanted to."

"Sometimes you need to run. Sometimes running away, sometimes running toward things. Life is not about standing still." He dumped the last load of snow of the roof, and began sweeping the last solar panel. "What would you do if I threw a snowball at you?"

He wouldn't miss, that was for sure. "I'd lob one right back," she said.

"Yet I am bigger than you, with better aim. This is a fight you cannot win," he said. He was already onto the next panel. He even swept faster than she did.

"Depends on what you mean by winning. I'd consider one good hit to the face or the groin a win," she said. She swallowed. God, what was she saying? She was his boss. She wasn't supposed to hurt him. There were laws about these things.

"So you would continue to fight an opponent, no matter what the outcome? That is both stubborn and brave. Very Viking traits. You are well suited to life here."

Freyja burst out laughing. "Yeah, if it wasn't for all the snow." She looked up, to find he'd cleaned off the last panel. They were finished.

Yet...she didn't want to go inside yet. She

eyed the remaining pile of snow at her feet. "Hey, Olaf, do you want to build a snowman?"

TWENTY

They build three snowmen, at the farthest corner of the roof from the raven family, for Odin had left their snowdrift shelter untouched. Freyja found leaves and sticks to give the men faces, and Odin was struck with the memory of the last time he'd made men out of snow.

It was the last night he'd seen his sons alive. Vali had been bitter, slinking off to sulk when

Odin refused to take the boy raiding with him. Vidarr, the more persuasive of the two, had tried to get him to stay home, instead of leading his men. Odin had suggested they build Vidarr his own army of snowmen to defend them while he was gone.

He'd given them faces and weapons and even armour made of sticks and leaves, and they'd still been standing, surrounding the house, when he'd arrived home. But they'd been poor defenders, because his family had not survived the attack.

Odin fell to his knees, nearly toppling the last snowman, which was the same height Vidarr had been, when he'd last seen him. Round as a ball in his winter clothes, just like the snowman. Oh, by all the gods…if he'd loved Frigg more, would he have stayed? Would he have been able to save them?

A hand landed lightly on his shoulder. "Olaf? Are you all right?"

What must she think of him? Some protector, sniffling and weeping in the snow.

"I was thinking of the last time I saw my son. When we built snowmen together."

Her voice was dull, flat. "I'm so sorry for your loss." Her arms came around him, hugging him, heedless of his tears or his weakness. Offering her own strength. Something no one had ever offered him before.

He fell in love with her all over again.

TWENTY-ONE

Snow started to fall in earnest, bringing Freyja to her senses. What the hell was she doing hugging Olaf on the roof?

She'd lost count of the times she'd counselled grieving or soon to be grieving families in hospital, but not once had she ever been unprofessional enough to hug someone. Okay, most of the time they'd looked like they wanted to strangle her for being the bearer of bad news, which had made it easier, and she hadn't slept with any of her patients' families like she had with Olaf, but…

Oh god, if he'd had a son, that probably meant he had a wife, too. Which made their nights of hot sex even worse.

Freyja mumbled something about going inside, and quickly moved away from Olaf, back into the relative warmth of the building. Warmth that would dissipate quickly until the power kicked back in, or sunlight hit the solar panels in the morning.

She and Olaf would just have to snuggle up for another night together. And if it was anything like the last two nights…

Her cheeks burned at the thought. No. She was not getting naked with Olaf again. The first night, she hadn't known who he was, so it was kind of excusable, but last night…last night was never to be repeated. Ever.

She'd left the lanterns on the roof, so she used her phone flashlight to guide her to the kitchen. The pizza had been hours ago, and it was probably dinnertime by now. With no power, she'd have to scrounge for something in the store rooms that didn't need cooking. She vaguely remembered seeing jars of pickled herring and tins of sardines, neither of which appealed to her.

Maybe she should just go for some liquid bread, she thought, reaching into one of the beer cartons. That's what ancient people had called beer, hadn't they? Instead of cans, though, her hand closed around something plastic and crackly — a bag of barbeque flavoured chips. Beer and chips, then, she decided, digging around until she found a can as well.

She took her plunder back to the cafeteria, which was now lit by the lanterns Olaf had brought down from the roof. He just sat there, his arms folded on the table, looking at her.

She should have thought to grab him a beer, too. "There's more beer in the store room. Proper food, too, though most of the stuff that doesn't need to be cooked is fish."

Olaf shook his head. "I am not hungry."

Freyja didn't think she was, either, but she opened the chips and popped a couple in her mouth, just to stop herself from saying something stupid. Then she cracked open her beer, taking a long pull from the can, before setting it down firmly on the table. God, that stuff was awful. Worse than some of the stuff she'd drunk as a student back home. She'd preferred fruity premixes back then, but the last time she'd had one of them was…Halloween, the holiday she now hated more than any other day on the calendar.

She should tell him. He'd told her about losing his son, so she should tell him her whole sordid story. What she was really running away from, though she'd since learned there was nowhere in the world she could run to where they didn't know, or wouldn't find out. Better than Olaf heard it from her than Saint Nik, though he was in hospital, wasn't he? He'd be out soon enough, and seeing as he was the one who'd told everyone else on campus, he'd probably get a kick out of telling Olaf, too.

"I used to be a doctor. Well, I finished my degree, and my internship, and I was well into my residency at a big city hospital. I hadn't decided what I wanted to specialise in. I was leaning toward emergency medicine, but my dad kept telling me I should become an anaesthetist, because the demand was so high for them, and putting people to sleep had to be way easier than triage when everything's crazy and happening at once…" She couldn't help smiling a little at the memory. That was what she'd liked most about medicine. Not all the study and memorising stuff, but the way her mind would go calm in all the chaos and she could make split second decisions and know she'd made the right call. Calls she would never make again, because of him.

"Anyway…I was on rotation in the oncology ward. I absolutely hated it there, because for every person who'd had their tumour or whatever successfully removed, there were half a dozen others who weren't so lucky. People whose lives were suddenly cut short by a random cell abnormality that just wouldn't die. We'd fight them in every way possible, with every weapon modern medicine could provide, even nuclear ones, and it still wasn't enough. Cancer is like cockroaches, I swear. Just when you think you've killed it, a dozen more pop up, livelier than ever, while the poor person knows they're going to die. And when you're the doctor, you have to tell them. You have to give them the bad news that they're not going to make it. That you can't work miracles or magic and they're going to die.

"Some people were really good at it. Some even made a career out of hospice medicine. Once girl I knew, this calm serene sort of person you just knew was some sort of saint, told me you had to think of it as end of life care. Just like newborns had midwives to usher them screaming into this world, some people needed someone to be there to usher them out of it with as much dignity and kindness as they deserved. And they do and I know she's right and I hope she's still doing a fucking amazing job with her terminal patients and that she can do it for a really long time, but that wasn't me. Death was like the ultimate failure to me. Patients would come to hospital for help and I felt like such a fucking failure if I couldn't help them.

"It was even worse when we got kids, or young people. People the same age as me, looking at the pointy end of death when they should have decades of life ahead of them. The parents were worse – they looked like zombies, desperate for a miracle they knew couldn't come, utterly horrified that they were going to outlive their kids. Which shouldn't happen, you know?"

Olaf nodded gravely.

Right. He did know. Better than anyone.

"Anyway, that year, Halloween was on the weekend, and my roommate decided she wanted to throw a party. She'd been assigned to the maternity ward, but we both managed to get our rosters to match so we'd be free that night. She did a lot of night shifts, so she finished before I did, and she came to remind me about the party. I was doing my final rounds of my patients for the shift, dragging my feet a bit, and she caught me in the room of a patient who hadn't been conscious for days. The doctor in charge said he wouldn't last until morning, so I knew someone else would be in his bed when I came back to work the next day, but I just wanted to take a minute…I don't know, to say goodbye or I'm sorry or whatever it was you said to the people you failed to save.

"So she came into the patient's room with me, reminded me what time the party started, and to make sure I picked a few last minute items up on my way home. I said I would, and then I picked up the patient's chart to record my last set of observations. I had to lift up the death certificate to do it – the doctor had already put it in there, signed it with the day's date and everything, which just made me want to cry for this guy I didn't know. But when I put the chart down, I found him staring at me. This bloke who couldn't have been any older than I was.

"And he said, 'I wouldn't mind being your date for the party. I've never been to a Halloween party before.'

"I looked at him and he looked at me, and something unspoken passed between us, that all the things he hadn't done, he never would now. So I blathered something about hospital procedures and how he was in safe hands here in hospital and how parties weren't all they were cracked up to be, because I'd be mopping up vomit by morning, for sure. He just nodded like he understood, and I left. I just left."

She stared hard at the beer can. She couldn't meet Olaf's gaze now, or she'd cry. She was probably going to cry anyway by the time this story was over, but now she'd started, she had to finish it.

"So I finished handover, stopped at the shops, and went home. The house was full of people, inside and in the backyard, and maybe I had a few more drinks than I should have. Someone had invited some firestick twirlers, and everyone went outside to watch them, so I curled up on the couch, just for a minute. It'd been a long day and a long week, and I'd had a bit to drink, so I fell asleep.

"The party ended. My roommate got called in to work because babies like being born at stupid o'clock in the morning, and she just sort of tiptoed out without waking anyone or checking on anyone because we were all supposed to be responsible adults, or adults, anyway, and everyone else was still asleep.

"So I woke up, on the couch, mid morning, with a slight hangover, but nothing too bad. There was a guy there, too, using my legs as a pillow, who'd fallen asleep on the other end of the couch. We're all fully clothed, nothing dodgy, so I just sort of slid my legs out from under him, letting him flop onto the couch as I got up.

"I don't know what it was. Whether he just

didn't fall right or maybe I saw his face first or…I don't know. So I reached out, to feel for a pulse. And it wasn't there. The guy was dead.

"I screamed for someone to call an ambulance, and I laid him down on the floor, so I could start doing compressions. But even as I did, I knew it was no use. He was cold, and his skin was kind of grey, and even my alcohol fogged brain was telling me he was a corpse, but I kept up those compressions until the ambulance arrived to take him away.

"It wasn't until about an hour later that I realised I knew him. He was the guy from the hospital. The patient I had definitely left behind in his room, who should not have been in my house, let alone on my couch. That's also about the time his parents turned up at the hospital, having rushed home from some remote hiking trip, absolutely hysterical that they weren't in time to say one last goodbye to their darling son. But when the hospital went looking for his body…well, it wasn't in the morgue, now, was it? So his parents raised absolute fucking hell, calling everyone from the cleaners to the consultants incompetent, until they got a call that he'd been taken to the state mortuary for an autopsy, and they needed to come and identify him.

"The police got involved, hospital administration got involved. Every newspaper and reporter in the city turned into terriers, trying to bite my heels in search of the story. Never mind that it was my roommate who'd given him our address, not me, or that he'd discharged himself from hospital, gotten into a taxi and invited himself into my house to crash my Halloween party, before collapsing on my couch to breathe his last. No, he was my patient, and people had taken pictures of us on the couch together, and the news got hold of all of it…

"They called me the fucking Body Thief, because he'd entered a time on his own death certificate when he left the hospital, that said he was already dead by the time he got into that cab, so the newspapers said I'd stolen his corpse. Someone said it was for necrophilia, while others said he was a macabre Halloween decoration, and I don't remember the rest. The police even came and arrested me as a fucking murder suspect. The hospital fired me. All because some selfish wanker called Amal wanted to spend the last hours of his life at my party."

Freyja wiped away her tears with her hands. Even now, it was still so fucking frustrating. All so unfair. She hadn't done anything wrong, except have a few adult beverages at her own house and fall asleep on her own couch. While Amal had just quietly died, and left her in the middle of a fucking shitstorm.

"The police dropped the charges, eventually, after they found the cab driver who'd driven Amal to my house, because his story backed mine up, and so did the autopsy. But it was already too late for me — between the media storm and the hospital's very public condemnation of my actions, stirred up by Amal's angry parents...I had no job, and no one was willing to hire the Body Thief.

"For a week, I hid at home, scouring the job boards for something I could do, somewhere I could go where no one had heard about it. Finally, I saw this job advertised – Karl was leading an expedition to the Jotunheimen Mountains, and he needed someone with experience in dissections to manage the lab here. I was the only one who applied with a medical degree, so he hired me on the spot. I scraped together some money for a plane ticket, and caught the next flight out."

Freyja blew out a breath. She picked up her beer to take another swig, only to discover it was empty. "So now I'm going to get drunk for the first time since that night, because as soon as the snow clears, the police are going to come here, and probably arrest me again, because the body of a thousand year old Viking that Karl entrusted to me is missing, and I have no fucking idea where it is. But because everyone knows I'm the Body Thief, everyone's going to blame me for it going missing. Just like last time. And when I lose my job this time…I don't know what I'll do."

She glanced up, to find she'd been talking to herself. Olaf was gone.

TWENTY-TWO

Odin could not help but be mesmerised by Freyja. As her words flowed, she occasionally paused to take a swig from her ale, before she pursed her lips as though she did not like the taste. Every time she did this, Odin wanted to lean forward and kiss her, but he dared not interrupt. This telling was too important to her. She had given him a hug when he'd needed it most; he would do her the same courtesy, and give her his full attention for as long as she needed it.

There was much in Freyja's tale that Odin did not understand, but he could certainly sympathise with her trying to heal a man, only to lose him to illness, and then be accused of his murder. Never mind that she'd been found innocent…he could not have lived among people who would believe such a thing of him, either.

He'd been on the brink of saying so, when she'd mentioned the missing body of the thousand year old Viking.

A thousand years…

His mind had gone blank.

Was that why he understood so little of the world around him? The witch had made him sleep for a thousand years.

Only to wake, frozen, on Freyja's metal table, to both save her and turn her life upside down.

His feet carried him swiftly out of the feasting hall and down to the lab, as she called it, where he'd first awoken. He could not pass through the walls to enter the cold storage chamber, but the stone floors yielded to him.

He lay down on the table again, in the tub of icy water, and remembered. The chill in his bones from being frozen for a thousand years. His spear, all that was left of his things, after all this time, for no tunic or cloak or boots survived that long.

He almost wished he could return to that unknowing slumber, no longer beset by his crushing grief for Vali and Vidarr, or the guilt at not having loved Frigg better. Or the loss of his men, leading them against Erik when he knew how vast the man's armies were, yet also knowing his men would choose to die in battle, avenging their families, so that they might see them in Valhalla, rather than live under Erik's rule.

All but Thor and Loki. If he'd known he was bargaining not just his own life in service to the man who'd killed his family, but a thousand years of sleep for the lives of his two remaining brothers in arms…he would do it again.

And Freyja? Where did she fit in all of this?

Erik's witch had commanded him to rise when she called, but Freyja was not that witch. Yet it was her call for help that had awoken him…she who compelled him to love her, to obey…was this some sort of sorcery, too?

No, he decided. Freyja was not a witch, for all that she enchanted him. Love was a magic all its own, and he knew what he felt for her just as he knew he'd never loved Frigg…and he would never stop loving his lost sons. Not even if he lived another thousand years.

But a lot could happen in a thousand years. More than he could learn about in any maintenance manual. Perhaps he should have paid more attention to the other books in Freyja's scriptorium. The chamber where she slept, so he must hurry if he meant to borrow some of the books before she retired for the evening.

Warming her bed was a wondrous thing, but

he needed to understand her world so that he could properly protect her. If that meant reading every book she had, then he would do so…and he would not return to her bed until he deserved her trust.

TWENTY-THREE

Freyja finished the chips, chasing them down with a cup of water, because she definitely didn't want another foul beer. When Olaf still didn't return, and her eyes grew heavy, she decided to go to bed, taking one of the lanterns with her. If Olaf was right, the solar panels would start working again when the sun rose, and there would be power in the building again. Light and heat and, most importantly, power for the coffee maker.

She half hoped to find him in the bed they'd shared last night, keeping it warm, for it was going to be a cold night, without any power. But the library was cold and empty, so she stole a bunch of spare blankets from one of the guest rooms to help keep her warm through the night.

He had to return eventually. Where else would he go?

Then again, now he'd heard her dark secret, maybe he didn't want to share a bed with her, not even to keep warm. She remembered the horror in Saint Nik's eyes when he'd mentioned the rumours of necrophilia – and he was a man who went after any woman on campus. But he kept well away from her.

Could she blame him, really? Even if she hadn't been guilty of any crime, she was still a disgraced doctor, one no hospital or clinic would employ. It was only a matter of time before she became a disgraced lab manager, too.

If she could find somewhere else to sleep, far from all her failures, she would, too.

She shucked off her jacket and her shoes, but left the rest of her clothes on for warmth, before burrowing under the blankets.

But instead of her body warming them, the blankets only seemed to chill her further, stealing all her body heat until the chill invaded her very bones. It never got this cold back home.

Had she made a mistake in coming here? Running halfway around the world to get away, when the rumours had still followed her?

She'd hoped for a fresh start, and for a time, she'd had one. Until the rumours had arrived, more virulent than any virus, so that not even the office sleaze would dare touch her. Not that she'd wanted attention from Saint Nik, especially when rumour had it he preferred students and people he had power over, and he'd learned quickly that making false complaints about her wouldn't fly. She might be a disgraced doctor, but no one knew better than a medical professional how well good documentation could cover even the most sizeable arse. Amal's wrongly dated death certificate had been her downfall, and it wasn't a mistake she'd ever repeat.

Maybe she should have stayed home, where it was warm. She might not be able to practice as a doctor again, but there were surely some public health positions in dire need of experts right now.

If her father really could pull some strings…

She sighed, her breath condensing in the air. Fuck, it was cold. She'd give anything for Olaf to share her bed again tonight. Just for warmth. Nothing else, no matter how much she wanted it.

She should never have told him her story. Especially not tonight. If there was any chance he might trip and bump his head, so he forgot the last few hours…

No. She wouldn't wish that on anyone. Head injuries were tricky things, with complications that could go on for weeks or months or even years, undetected.

Maybe she was the damaged one, and she could blame all her bad decisions over the last few days on hitting her head when she'd lost control of the scooter, just before she'd met Olaf. If she could blame a head injury for all of her mistakes since then…

No. Not even a head injury would explain away the missing body. Better for the injury to have been fatal, and she'd never know the consequences of her second fall from grace.

Because she wasn't sure she had the strength to start over a third time.

Maybe…maybe it was best that the power was out, and she was freezing. If she succumbed to hypothermia tonight, no one would blame her for anything. Just like no one had dared pin the rightful blame on Amal for signing his own death certificate and escaping hospital to go to a party, of all things.

Was this how easy it had been for Amal? Just falling asleep, knowing you'd never wake up and have to face any consequences for your actions?

She'd always felt sorry for him, when she hadn't been furious at him, wishing she could raise him from the dead so she could kick him in the fork for fucking up her life. Selfish arsehole.

But right now, being selfish seemed like a really good idea. Slipping away so someone else could be held responsible for everything, just for once. Maybe they'd blame Olaf for the power outage, and he'd magically produce the missing body out of guilt.

Then again, if she was really being as selfish as Amal, she'd want one more night with Olaf. One last almighty orgasm.

She drifted off to sleep, dreaming about what she wanted, but didn't dare have.

TWENTY-FOUR

Odin heard Freyja's call as clearly as though she was sitting beside him, close enough to read the pages of the book he'd picked up. But no matter how much he longed to answer it, to join her in bed for all the delights her body could provide, he knew he hadn't earned that privilege yet.

He had a thousand years of history to catch up on. Maybe more, if he judged this history book correctly. He estimated he'd entered his enchanted sleep more than twelve hundred years ago, before the death of Karl the Great, the emperor the book called Charlemagne. More interesting was the lack of reference to Jarl Erik and his conquests, though Erik had been no less ambitious. He couldn't help but wonder what had erased Erik from history's record, while Karl remained.

Finally, he finished reading the books he had, and ventured back to the scriptorium for some more. He did not need sleep, like Freyja, but he took a moment to check on her, all the same.

Only to discover he'd been a fool. Yes, there were many dangers in this strange future he must protect her from, but some things did not change. The cold could kill just as readily now as it did in his time – and he would never have been careless enough to allow Frigg or his sons to sleep in such chilly conditions.

For as Freyja slept, she shivered – something he could not, in conscience, allow to continue.

He slipped beneath the blankets, taking her in his arms, even breaking out his wings to wrap around her, to warm her. She was softness itself, fitting into his embrace so perfectly, it was like he'd been made for her. Or she'd been made for him.

He breathed in her scent. Her hair smelled of some sort of fruit he did not recognise, but as his lips hovered over the nape of her neck, desperate to drop a kiss there, her scent grew saltier, yet also sweeter. Like she'd bathed in honey before going out on the roof with him to clear off the snow.

Maybe that was why she tasted so very sweet…

He dropped a kiss in the air above her neck, resisting every urge to offer her more. It would be so easy to slide down her trousers, to slip inside her wet heat, and warm her from the inside as well, as he gave her a thousand kisses.

But he did not, though he was harder than the living stone he was made of by the time she was warm, and he forced himself to leave her bed, taking another stack of books to occupy his mind so that he might better protect her. Only when he properly understood this world he'd awoken in, would he be able to truly protect her as she deserved.

Until he could protect her from every possible threat while she slept would he permit himself to surrender to her pleasure when she woke.

Protecting her should be motive enough for his studies, but more than once, Odin allowed his body to follow his wandering mind to her bed, where he might bury himself inside her and revel in every clench as her muscles tightened around him, while she screamed for joy. But all he did was make sure she was warm enough before forcing himself back to his books.

He would share this joy with her again, he promised himself, as he turned his eyes to the page, to read what he had not yet learned.

TWENTY-FIVE

The library was surprisingly warm when Freyja woke up. Or maybe that was just her makeshift bed on the floor, with so many blankets piled on top of her, it took considerable effort to climb out from under them.

Yes, definitely the blankets, keeping the warmth in, she decided, pulling on her jacket. Sure, her breath wasn't condensing the moment it left her mouth any more, but this was hardly a typical summer morning temperature. Even a Norwegian one.

She headed back to her room for some clothes, and the way the temperature dropped as she entered the accommodation block, she almost began to believe the place might be haunted. It would be funny if it was the ghost of the guy whose body was supposed to be sitting in the necropsy freezer – they could look for his lost body together.

Though it was unlikely they'd find it before the university PR team and the police arrived.

This might be her last morning as a free woman.

So she took her time in the shower, now the hot water was working again, and debated whether she should use the last of the bread to make toast, or go for something more fancy, as her last meal here and all. Wait, was that pancake mix? She grabbed the packet. Yep, the sort that you only needed to add water, to, so even she couldn't stuff them up.

While the frying pan heated up, she dug out

syrup and butter – no way was she eating margarine today if she'd be eating prison rations for the foreseeable future. She methodically poured, flipped, plated, then poured again, methodically making a stack of pancakes that would easily last her 'til lunch, and still there was way too much batter for one person.

If Olaf was around, she'd offer to make some for him, too, seeing as he was probably responsible for getting the backup power up and running again, but she hadn't seen any sign of him.

Maybe he was already outside with the snow blower, clearing the way for the police to come and arrest her.

So she shouldn't waste her last hour of freedom making pancakes for the traitor.

Unless…making it easier for the police to come and get her put them in a better mood, and maybe they'd be nicer, or decide not to bother with handcuffs. Then again, with the university PR team here, including a photographer, her face would probably be splashed across all the newspapers again whether she wore handcuffs or not.

Was it too late to contact Ingrid and tell her not to come? The police would turn up anyway, of course, but if she told Ingrid the body was missing, then maybe she wouldn't have to face the photographer. Small mercies…

She fetched her laptop and opened it on the cafeteria table, making herself a second coffee while she waited for the wifi connection to start working and load the emails that had come in while the power and the wifi were down.

Amid the mess of spam and the usual generic notices from the university was an email from Ingrid, dated yesterday.

Apparently, the roads were closed, due to the unseasonable snow, so neither Ingrid nor the police would be able to get to the lab before next week, at the earliest. Was there any chance she could delay working on the body until then, so the police forensics team could have the first stab at it?

Freyja wasn't sure whether she wanted to laugh or cry. Sure, she could absolutely keep her hands off the body…because she had no idea where the fucking thing was. But the snow had bought her a week's reprieve. What was the legal term for it? A stay of execution? Not that they had the death penalty here in Norway or back home either, but last time it had felt like her life ending, and she knew this time would be no different.

She tapped out a vague email, agreeing to see Ingrid and whoever else was coming next week. What more could she say? She was stuck here, awaiting her fate, at least until the snow melted.

What she needed was a miracle.

What she had was Olaf, a massive lab facility, and a whole lot of snow. And a week left of life as she knew it.

Well, if she only had a week left…she might as well make a bucket list.

She pulled up a blank page on her laptop screen and began to type.

1. Find the ice mummy and put it back in the fridge.

Well, it was her priority, even if it was a long shot.

Then again, how had they lured the mummy back into his tomb, in that old movie? Freyja had a bad feeling a girl had sacrificed herself to be bait or something, and Freyja would take prison over seducing some long-dead Viking any day. No matter what the news or the rumours said, she was NOT into necrophilia.

All she'd heard about Viking culture was that they loved their food – and their idea of heaven was a feasting hall in the sky. So…maybe a trail of fish would be better bait. They definitely had enough sardines and herring here to lure anyone from the road all the way to the necropsy lab, if need be. Fuck knew she wasn't going to be eating them, especially now the power was back on. Even if they ran out of normal food, or if the power went out again, she could take one of the portable gas burners the expeditioners used and some of their dehydrated meals out into the courtyard and have a cookout.

Last year, even Lara had admitted those meals weren't bad, though they couldn't beat fresh food. Fish, however…

Freyja buried her head in her hands. She must be going mad, if she was actually considering this. Ice mummies, like any other mummified remains, didn't move, wouldn't respond to any kind of bait, virginal, piscine or otherwise, and, most importantly, couldn't get up and walk out of a fridge without someone carrying them out.

So it wasn't the mummy she was trying to bribe, but the thief, which still left her with the problem that even a year's worth of smoked herring still wouldn't work.

Freyja blew out a breath. Well, if she couldn't achieve the first item on her list, she needed more things she could actually tick off.

2. Pancakes for breakfast every morning

3. Hawaiian pizza every day

4. Another orgasm with Olaf

Freyja stretched for the delete key. She shouldn't even be thinking about him. Then again, if she was going to lose her job anyway because she failed to achieve the first item on the list, then she may as well do some bad things that weren't likely to land her in prison.

She put her pinky back where it belonged on the keyboard, so she could add more to the list.

5. Another night with Olaf

6. Destroy the sundial

7. Drink the bottle of champagne Karl had had delivered with the ice mummy

He'd had a whole case of it sent to the expedition site, but he'd insisted on her having a bottle, too. She'd planned on drinking it with the team or at least Karl when he got back, but now…she might as well guzzle the lot on her own.

8. Eat the last pack of Tim Tams

She'd brought a bunch in her suitcase with

her, and she'd been saving the last packet for a special occasion. Better to eat them now than let them go bad while she was in prison. Maybe she should try to seduce Olaf with them...

Maybe if she was really lucky, she wouldn't go to prison, and they'd just cancel her visa and deport her back to Australia. Then she could eat all the Tim Tams she wanted, while looking for another job. Though who would employ her after this, she had no idea.

In the meantime, she intended to check if there were enough pineapple pizzas to achieve goal number three.

TWENTY-SIX

Odin closed the last book, and slipped through the walls to return it to its shelf. He'd taken to travelling this way in order to avoid Freyja, and the temptation that came with being too close to her. Oh, he watched over her, and if she called for help, he could be almost instantly by her side, but the more he read, the more certain he became of two things.

Firstly, that so much had changed in the

world while he'd been asleep, that it would take him a lifetime to learn enough to live in the world as it was now.

Secondly, that he had no hope of defending Freyja from all the things he barely understood in this world, so he definitely didn't deserve the title of being her protector at all.

And if he could not protect her, then he did not deserve to share her bed. No matter how much he longed to.

For if he lost her the way he'd lost Frigg, Vali and Vidarr, he could not live with himself.

He had to tell her. He'd promised to protect her, and if he failed to keep that promise…he needed to ask her to release him from his obligation, so that she might find a modern man, from her own time, who could protect her as she deserved, and love her as she deserved. Not just the latter.

Odin took a deep breath and marched into the feasting hall where Freyja usually was at this time of day, eating a salty-sweet flatbread topped with something pink and yellow.

"Would you like a slice of pizza?" she asked, pushing the platter toward him.

Odin shook his head. "I am not hungry." He almost wished it were not so, so that he might share a meal with her, or share every meal with her, but this was part of the curse Erik's witch had cast on him. A spell that should have made him strong enough to protect the woman he loved from anything…except a future no one could have foreseen.

Freyja smiled sadly. "You're just being polite, aren't you? No one else likes pineapple on their pizza, either. There's still plenty of other kinds in the freezer. Pepperoni, supreme, and maybe even a couple of the Moroccan lamb ones that are way too spicy for me. I might switch it up a bit and try something else tomorrow, though. Having the same pizza every day, even when it's my favourite, can be a bit much. Then again, I'm sure I'll miss it next week, when I'm not here any more."

If Odin's heart had still been beating, it

would have stood still in his chest. "You are leaving?"

"Not willingly. But when the police arrive on Monday morning and they discover the body's missing, they'll arrest me for sure."

As her story spilled out, some of it the same things she'd said the other night, and some of it entirely new, he began to understand more of it.

These police would bring her to face justice, for the loss of the body in the cold storage chamber. His body, and his fault it was missing. Not hers.

She would be exiled – maybe for a short time, but most likely for much longer – and not allowed to return to her work here.

He'd placed her life and her livelihood at stake, simply by answering her call for help.

If he'd only had the sense to ignore her call, to acknowledge that he was such a poor protector that another man would be better suited to help her, she would not be in this predicament. This was his fault, yet she would be the one to suffer for it. Just like Frigg.

He had to fix this. Find a way to set things right. Before the police came to take her away.

If he only had the courage to do it.

He stared at her, allowing himself to feel all the longing he'd pushed down deep inside over the last few days. He would do anything for Freyja.

But he would wait until she fell asleep. He'd steal one more evening of her time, before he gave her up forever.

"What are your plans for this evening?" Freyja asked.

He swallowed. Oh, he was such a coward. "I'd hoped I might spend this evening with you."

Her eyes lit up. "Wonderful! You see, I have this list, and there are a couple of things on it I'd like your help with."

Odin inclined his head. "Whatever you wish, I am yours to command." For one last night.

TWENTY-SEVEN

Whatever she wished. Freyja couldn't suppress a little shiver of anticipation at those words. She couldn't remember anyone saying them to her before. Not even when she'd gotten top marks in her final exams at high school, giving her a university entry rank that would allow her to choose any university course she wanted…as long as it was medical, like the rest of her family.

After her brother had chosen dentistry instead of medicine, saying it had better hours and better money, World War III had still raged in their household for weeks, followed by a Cold War that still erupted every Christmas. She hadn't expected to be home for Christmas this year, but now…

Freyja sighed. Before she could really let her imagination run wild and start wishing, she had to know the truth. She took a deep breath.

"First, I need to ask you one question, and I need you to be completely honest with me. There's no chance you sort of accidentally took a body from the necropsy fridge and maybe just buried it in the snow outside, and then sort of forgot where you put it, right? Because if you did, and you happened to find it again while you're clearing out the courtyard, and put the body back in the fridge, no one else would ever know." Her voice got a bit squeaky at the end, as desperation crept in. If the body came back, she wouldn't need her pre-prison bucket list, and everything could go back to normal. Sure, she wouldn't be able to sleep with Olaf again, but…

Olaf's huge hands clasped her shoulders. Firm and reassuring, but still gentle. "Doctor Freyja, you are absolutely right. There are no bodies buried outside in the snow, forgotten or otherwise. But I promise you, I will do everything in my power to help you find the one you are looking for, so that, as you say, no one will ever know it was missing." Sincerity beamed out of his one blue eye, almost electric in its intensity.

She'd known he wasn't a thief, but that he believed he could find the body, when she'd all but given up…maybe that was why he was the one person she'd miss most about this place. Because if she could choose to be snowed in or trapped on a deserted island with anyone again, she'd choose Olaf in a heartbeat.

Which was why she was determined to seduce him into her bed one more time before the police dragged her away from Icelab. She'd never seduced a man in her life, and was pretty certain she'd do a pretty clumsy job of it, but if she had only one wish…

"Want to share a bottle of champagne with me?" The words came out of her mouth before she could stop them.

Olaf shook his head slowly. "I do not drink."

Of course he didn't. A man with a body like his evidently treated it like a temple. No pizza, no pancakes, no alcohol…for him, all-night incredible sex was probably just another workout.

Unless he was a reformed alcoholic, which wouldn't be unreasonable, after he'd lost his kid.

Either way, she shouldn't have mentioned the champagne. The last time she'd drunk champagne was the night Amal had ruined her life.

Which meant she'd have to try and seduce him sober, which was going to be even worse and probably wouldn't work and she'd go to prison still wanting, with all the things on her

bucket list unticked and…
    Olaf captured her mouth with his.
    And Freyja forgot how to breathe.

TWENTY-EIGHT

"Please," she moaned, as he broke the kiss for only a moment to scoop Freyja up in his arms.

Then he was kissing her again as he strode through the corridors to the scriptorium she'd made her bedchamber. He'd studied the maintenance manual so that he might master the controls of the box on the wall, turning up the temperature until it resembled a summer's day instead of the depths of winter in here.

He started to help her out of her clothing, but the moment her breasts were bare, he could not help himself. He laid her down on the bed, so that he had both hands free to caress her. Silken softness itself, as always, except for her nipples, which were almost as hard as his own stone skin. Gods, and the taste…

She arched her back up, offering herself to him, as he took his time on first one breast, then the other, and he couldn't seem to stop his fingers from stroking her.

And the way she whimpered that one word, PLEASE, over and over. Gods, he could not refuse her anything. Instead, he would give her everything, and more.

She fumbled at the fastenings of her trousers, and Odin read her intention, as though the picture had popped from her mind to his.

He slid his hands down her back, into the back of her trousers, cupping the sweet globes of her arse, before squeezing just a little.

Another moan, another PLEASE, before he tugged off her trousers entirely, baring her whole body to him.

A small part of him wanted to thrust inside her and stay there until dawn, but he was too obsessed with the taste of her to do that just yet.

No, he knelt between her thighs, lifting her legs over his shoulders as he bowed over her, kissing her in the one place he longed for most. More heavenly than even Valhalla.

He tasted her with his lips, then with his tongue, before taking his hands to spread her out before him, so that he might explore every fold, every sensitive spot, as she moaned and squirmed beneath him.

"Oh, please!" she begged.

Slowly, he coaxed her to her first orgasm of the evening, pausing to taste her again and again as she grew wetter, her cries wilder. Finally, as he felt her clench around his fingers, he drank her very essence, as she cried out to the gods in ecstasy.

Sweeter than the finest mead, yet salty, too, as the best meads always were.

Intent on wringing more pleasure from her begging body, he dipped his head so that he might drink again.

TWENTY-NINE

Freyja might have sucked a couple of cocks in her life, but she'd never had a man go down on her. And Olaf…god, he was as good with his tongue as he was with the rest of his gorgeous body. If she had one wish, it would be to ride his face for eternity, but right now, he had her pinned to the bed, his face buried between her thighs, completely in control while she had none, and she wasn't sure what she liked more.

Especially when a second orgasm quickly followed the first, and a third one threatened to overwhelm her completely.

Oh god, he was going to give her a fourth. And a fifth…

She screamed and bucked and begged for more, taking everything he gave, while he drank her in, teasing and torturous and so fucking divine she wished this night could last forever.

After more orgasms than she thought her body could take, she blinked away her bliss from her umpteenth climax to find him staring down at her, desire burning in his eyes, now completely naked.

And his cock was…well, fucking massive, that was for sure. Almost bigger than she remembered, which made no sense, because it had fitted fine inside her before. Very fine, in fact.

He pulled her up, so she straddled his lap, his cock rubbing her folds, yet still not inside her.

"Please, Olaf. Please," she begged, grinding herself against him. Another orgasm shouldn't even be possible, and yet she could feel the pleasure building.

From that glint in his eye, she knew he felt it, too. He fasted his hands around her hips, pressing her down harder, still not entering her. "Come for me, Freyja," he ordered.

Suddenly she felt like she'd drunk the whole bottle of champagne anyway, pleasure bubbling up inside her until she couldn't help but scream.

And Olaf rewarded her, giving her every inch of his considerable cock until he was buried in her to the hilt, stretching her to her very limits. Or maybe even past them, she wasn't sure.

"Fuck. Fuck," she moaned, trying to adjust to his girth while still holding on to the last wisps of euphoria from that last orgasm.

Then he began to move inside her, glacial thrust after glacial thrust, though his touch was anything but icy. Setting her on fire from the inside out, with one hand burning against her hip, and the other branding her arse.

And his mouth was everywhere…her throat, her breasts, her lips, before he took one of her nipples in his teeth, biting down just hard enough to make her yelp, before sucking hard to soothe the sting.

And his cock? Fuck, she'd thought earlier that she'd like to ride his face…now, she wanted to sit in his lap forever. Impaling herself on him over and over until the impossible happened – another orgasm, building bigger than anything she'd ever known before, tonight or otherwise, threatening to carry her away, to bury her entirely, and she didn't care what it did, as long as Olaf didn't stop moving his massive cock and…

Oh

FUCKFUCKFUCKFUCKINGFUCK…

Before words left her altogether.

THIRTY

Sometime after midnight, Odin knew they should stop. Freyja was exhausted, so drunk on pleasure she could not sit upright in his lap any more if he did not support her, so he laid her down on the pillows, trying to memorise the sight of her blissful face so that he would never forget this night.

"Don't stop. Please don't stop," she begged.

He leaned forward to kiss her. "I'd happily

make love to you forever, and never stop, but you need sleep."

She grabbed his arse, squeezing the cheeks with surprising strength. "I can sleep when tonight's over. Right now, all I need is you."

Odin wanted to tell her she deserved so much more. A man who could protect her, who would put her needs before his own selfish ones, who had not almost cost her her livelihood…but buried in her wet heat, as he was right now, he could not resist her.

So he made love to her languidly, as though they had all the time in the world, while dawn crept irrevocably closer.

One final orgasm shuddered through her body, as her eyelids drooped. "I love you," she mumbled, as her eyes slid shut.

Odin's heart shattered within his chest, stone shards piercing his insides. "Not as much as I love you," he whispered, gently disengaging from her irresistible depths. He dropped one final kiss on her slightly parted lips, before gathering his things and heading to his own resting place.

He left the strange garment with Olaf's name on it, neatly folded on the same metal table where he'd found it. He'd already tipped the water out of the long tray that now only held his spear, but now he paused by the sink so that he might wash one more time, as was proper.

When he was clean, he opened the door of the cold storage room, barely feeling the chill as the air clouded around him. The tray on the wheeled table was cool against his skin, and long enough for him to stretch out to his full length, though his toes grazed the edge.

This was what Freyja needed, he told himself. A thousand year old Viking body in her cool room, not in her bed. For all that Odin wished it could be otherwise, he knew it could not. He could not.

Instead, he recalled her words, her last order to him: "Put the body back in the fridge. No one will ever know."

This was her command. As surely as her cry

for help had awoken him, her voice was the lullaby that would send him back into slumber.

Perhaps for another thousand years, and when he woke, no one would remember her name, or his, like the history books of this time that did not mention himself, or Erik, or any of his men.

But he would remember, and the memory would be his alone.

Smiling, Odin drifted into oblivion.

THIRTY-ONE

When Freyja woke and stumbled to the bathroom, she could barely walk. She probably shouldn't have had quite that much sex with Olaf, but he'd been so damn good and if it was the last time she ever got to…she'd be still riding him right now, if he was here. She'd never met a man with that kind of stamina — never met a man who lasted more than fifteen minutes, actually, let alone a dusk 'til dawn fuckfest that still left her aching for more.

They had time. The police weren't supposed to arrive until Monday, so there was still the rest of the weekend.

Maybe she could even entice Olaf into sharing a shower with her, she thought as she endured the lukewarm spray alone. If she could find him.

He'd left the library by the time she woke up, and he wasn't in the cafeteria, either.

The snow in the courtyard was starting to melt in the morning sun, she thought, or at least it looked like there was less of it, but there was no one else out there. It was almost like Olaf had left the lab entirely, which just wasn't possible. The driveway and the road all the way to the village were still as snowed in as ever, with no sign of shifting soon.

Unless a burst of summer weather came over the mountains, and melted it all away. That would still take days, though – time enough to do the last few things on her bucket list.

She donned her outdoor gear and headed

out into the courtyard, where she began to shape snowballs. One after the other, until she had a massive pile of them. Then she began to pelt the stupid sundial.

The first few throws went wide, or glanced off it, so she took a step closer, taking a second to aim before she let fly. When that one hit, the sundial rang faintly, like the echo of a bell. The faintest shadow of what Olaf could do, like trying to mop up a flood with a single tissue.

It wasn't fair. The world was full of selfish arseholes like Amal and Saint Nik and whoever had stolen Karl's ice mummy. Why did she always have to take the blame for it? Three snowballs hit the sundial, one after the other.

Didn't she work every bit as hard, if not harder?

She threw two snowballs this time, though only one hit the target.

Didn't she deserve to be happy?

The next one smashed against the plinth the sundial sat on, shattering into slush.

Didn't she deserve to have a career…

Pof!

…a hot man in her bed…

Pof!

…and for things to go right for once?

She threw missile after missile, until she ran out of snowballs, and had to make a fresh pile. She threw those, too, her aim growing steadily worse as it became harder and harder to see through the tears streaming down her face.

She should probably go inside before they froze, or worse, Olaf came back from his morning run, and saw her like this. He'd never touch her again if he knew what a fucking mess she was, compared to his hot perfection.

Maybe it was best that she'd be forced to leave before he found out how much of a failure she really was. She'd fucked up everything else in her life – she was certain she'd fuck up a relationship with him, too, if they had one. It was only a matter of time.

And seeing as he didn't drink…maybe she should go inside and have that bottle of champagne with breakfast. It wasn't like she could fuck things up any worse today.

Freyja trudged back to the loading dock, to shuck off her snow gear, before padding in her socks to the cafeteria.

THIRTY-TWO

"Thor, Loki, Odin. Come to my aid, for I have need of you."

Odin stirred in his cold, metal bed. The call was faint, but familiar. Not Freyja's beloved voice, but another's. Another whose call was stronger, though further away.

"Thor, Loki, Odin, wake and ready for battle, for I need your help."

It must be Erik's witch, the girl whose spell

had sent him to sleep for a thousand years. The one who'd cut out first Thor's heart, then Loki's. Yet if she was calling them, then they must still live.

Erik had kept his promise. Odin would not have believed it possible, for everything he knew about the man told him he was faithless, with no honour to speak of. Perhaps he'd been wrong.

Or perhaps it was the witch, and not Erik, honouring that promise. Odin had not known any witches, so he could not speak to their honour.

But if she kept faithfully to the oath he had made, then so must he. He'd vowed to answer the summons, when it came, and lead his men to victory in Erik's name.

Then again, more than a thousand years had passed. Erik could not possibly still live. How, then, was the witch still alive?

He had to answer. He had given his word. Erik might be faithless, but Odin still had some honour, for all his many mistakes.

"Thor, Loki, Odin, rise, for I summon you!"

No. Not yet, Odin thought. He had sworn to answer the summons, but he had never said when. He owed a debt to Freyja, too, who would be accused of theft if his body went missing before the police arrived. Therefore he must stay where he was, and return to his hibernation, until he knew Freyja was safe.

Then he might answer the witch's call. If she still called.

Satisfied, Odin slipped back into slumber.

THIRTY-THREE

Freyja raised her head from the cafeteria table, wishing it wouldn't hurt so much. Had she really drunk the whole bottle of champagne last night? She lifted the bottle and peered blearily inside. Well, someone definitely had, and there was no sign of Olaf.

At least she'd had the sense to have some cheese and crackers with it. But falling asleep on the plate of remaining cracker crumbs had not been part of her plan, because now she had crumbs stuck to her cheek and it was going to take a good scrub in front of a mirror or maybe a shower to get those off.

Not to mention she needed something to sort her headache. Fuck.

She stumbled toward the guest rooms, headed for hers.

Faintly, she heard a rhythmic banging sound. It sounded like it came from behind one of the closed guest room doors. Which made no sense, because there was no one here but her and Olaf.

"Oh my god, Loki!" a female voice cried, faint but clear enough to make out the words.

Maybe someone had left their phone behind, and that was their ringtone. Either that, or Olaf was watching some sort of weird fantasy porn. If he was, she was definitely not walking in on that. Stumbling across her brother's porn collection had been horrifying enough. After all, she and her parents had believed him when he picked dentistry for the money and the hours. If she'd known there was a whole genre of kinky dentist porn out there…Freyja shuddered. She hadn't been able to stomach telling her parents.

She grabbed clean clothes and some paracetamol, and headed for the bathrooms.

Only to see the most perfect arse she'd ever beheld, flexing for all it was worth, as its owner pounded into some dark-haired girl he had pinned to the wall.

"Olaf?" she whispered. Well, it had to be, didn't it? No one else was here.

Except…where had the girl come from?

Fuck, her head hurt more than ever.

She stomped back to the cafeteria for some water to swallow the pills. A sensible person would probably just take her hangover to bed and sleep it off, but Freyja's building fury at Olaf wasn't going to let her rest until she'd kicked his absurdly hot arse.

Had he lied to her? Did he have a way to get out of here, and was he or his new fuck buddy the body thief she'd been searching for all along?

So she marched back to the bathroom, but had to slump down on the floor outside the door, because her head hurt too much. She should have raided the medical supplies for something stronger than paracetamol. She was capable of injecting herself with a safe dose of…something. Anything to make all this go away, at least for a few hours.

The door opened, and a pair of hairy legs that ended in a towel wrapped around his hips swaggered out the door.

Freyja scrambled to her feet. "You lying, cheating, fucking bastard!" she said, giving him a shove. Of course, that only made her lose her balance, so she tumbled into his arms instead. Perfect fucking Olaf caught her before she could fall. Of course he did.

"Sibyl tells me I am a terrible liar, and it would be dishonourable to cheat," the man said, in a voice that definitely wasn't Olaf's.

Freyja squinted up at him. He had long, fair hair like Olaf, and just as many muscles, but he definitely had two eyes, with no eye patch to be seen. He was younger, too, without the faint lines around his eye that Olaf had. He could have been Olaf's younger brother, maybe, but he wasn't Olaf.

He grinned. "But how can any man resist an invitation for fucking when it comes from a woman as enchanting as my wife?"

"Thor, who are you talking to?" The girl appeared at his side, combing her wet hair. She was even smaller than Freyja had thought.

Freyja straightened, wincing as her head gave her a warning twinge. "I'm Doctor Freyja Valdis, the manager of this facility. Who are you and how did you get here? We've been snowed in for a week, nothing in or out. Unless you left a sleigh with reindeer in the courtyard." She just shook her head, then wished she hadn't. She was never drinking champagne again.

Younger Olaf with Two Eyes clapped his hands. "That is exactly what I said as we were flying here! With so much snow, we should tame a couple of reindeer, but Sibyl would not allow it. As her superior, with your permission, I could do it, and show Sibyl exactly what she's missing."

Sibyl…that did sound familiar. Not that she was supposed to be here. "Sibyl? Aren't you one of the expeditioners? One of the Harald Medal winners? Shouldn't you still be up in the mountains with Karl and the rest of his team?" But he'd said they'd flown, hadn't he? God, she'd slept through a helicopter landing. Never, ever having champagne again.

The girl grinned. "Yep, that's me. Jorunn's around here, too, but I think she's still in bed. Pretty sure she's awake, though. When we head back to site, we should probably take an extra tent. I mean, I don't mind sharing with her when it's just the two of us, but with you two as well…it could get a bit crowded."

Freyja blinked. So she hadn't imagined the noises she'd heard coming from that other guest room. Now she understood why Karl insisted on buying industrial sized boxes of condoms for the supply room. These expedition teams bonked like rabbits.

Of course, she and Olaf had used their fair share, but…

Sibyl waved her hand at the bathroom behind her, stirring up the steam into swirling eddies. "Anyway, the bathroom's all yours if you want it. I'm volunteering for breakfast duty, because if we let Jorunn do it, we'll end up with porridge or fish, and I for one am definitely sick of both of those." She marched off down the corridor like she knew exactly where she was going, with the nearly naked Thor trailing behind her.

THIRTY-FOUR

The scent wafting out of the cafeteria lured Freyja as surely as any mythical siren song. God, the place hadn't smelled this good since the end of expedition feast Lara had made at the end of last season. Had Lara come back, too?

But she found Sibyl in the kitchen, with a now fully clothed Thor leaning against the wall, just watching her work.

"These are savoury muffins. They don't need anything on them except maybe butter, egg or cheese," Sibyl said, setting the tray of muffins on the bench.

Thor held out the jar. "That's only because you haven't tried them with lingonberry jam. It's perfect on bread or roast meat. You put smoked pork in those, yes? So the jam will go perfectly. Butter and jam, my sister would insist."

Sibyl rolled her eyes. "Look, these muffins are made to my cousin's recipe. She runs the most amazing café back home, and no one beats her breakfasts, or her muffins. And if she says they are good enough the way they are, no way am I taking advice from some backward Viking who hasn't even tasted them." She turned to Freyja. "Please tell this dude from the dark ages that we don't do weird shit like eat cheese and bacon muffins with jam."

Thor folded his arms across his chest, just as stubborn as his wife. "You only say that because you have not tasted it before. If you had, you would agree with me. My sister is undoubtedly eating fare just like this in Valhalla as we speak."

"I can't believe you'd bring your sister into this. Fine. I'll sacrifice one muffin to this stupidity. I'll cut it up into small pieces, so no one has to endure your jam-contaminated abomination for more than a single bite. We'll each take one bite with jam, and one without." She lifted imploring eyes to meet Freyja's. "You'll help me with this experiment, won't you? Additional data points and all that?"

Anything to get her hands on one of those muffins. "All right, but I give you fair warning: I don't like lingonberry jam on anything."

Sibyl butchered and buttered the muffin, before Thor added a small dollop of jam to two pieces. "I'll leave the jar here in case you want more," he said, looking smug.

Sibyl rolled her eyes again. "Remind me again why I married you? Or handfasted, or whatever."

Thor's smile grew even more smug, if that

were possible. "Because you love me."

Sibyl hooked her foot around a rubbish bin and dragged it over to the bench. "If this tastes as horrible as I think it will, no judgement if you spit it out." She grabbed one of the jam morsels, and motioned for Freyja to do the same.

"Why aren't you having any?" Freyja asked, jerking her chin toward Thor. He might intimidate Sibyl with his size, but Freyja almost matched him for height. She wasn't scared of him.

"He's not hungry," Sibyl taunted, as though this was an old argument between them.

Thor bobbed his head. "As my wife says."

That was…weird. But Freyja didn't have time to think about it, because Sibyl had started counting down from three, and she had agreed to do this.

"Three, two, one…go!"

Freyja popped the piece into her mouth. Tartness hit her tongue, then salt and…actually, that wasn't bad. It almost reminded her of pineapple pizza, except without the tomato because you didn't need it with all those berry flavours bursting out everywhere.

Freyja swallowed. "That's not bad." She reached for a buttered piece. It was good, but a bit bland after the one with jam.

"Ugh, no thank you. You can keep the jam away from my muffins," Sibyl said, reaching for another one. "You can have as many as you like, though. The recipe's for the café, so I may have made a bigger batch than we need for three of us."

Thor just shook his head. "You, Doctor Freyja, are an honorary Viking, with taste to rival that of the greatest warriors in Valhalla. Whereas you, my wife…"

"I'm just married to one. Yeah, I know. Remind me to introduce you to Vegemite sometime. I think Hemsworth did an instructional video, too. You'll like that." Sibyl flicked her tea towel at him, before hanging it over the rail and turning her attention to the coffee maker.

"You must be Freyja!"

Arms came out of nowhere, wrapping Freyja in a tight hug from behind so she couldn't even see her assailant.

"Oh my god, Karl said you are the absolute queen of reindeer dissection. I can learn so much from you. When you're done dealing with Odin, I want to be right there in the lab with you, until you've taught me everything."

Tall, thin and blonde – Freyja's assailant might have been a Viking shieldmaiden, if she'd lived in those times. Her eyes shone with a frightening intensity that made Freyja think about berserkers. She couldn't suppress a slight shudder.

"And you are?"

The blonde's jaw dropped. "Shit. Sorry. I'm Jorunn. I'm the one who found Odin, which means I should probably be more excited about him than all the reindeer corpses, but Vikings are more Karl and Sibyl's thing, while I just do reindeer."

"And wolverines, and wolves, don't forget," said a male voice, as a new man stepped into the room, seizing Jorunn from behind so he could nuzzle her neck.

Freyja's head spun. If Thor was Olaf's younger brother, then this man was the baby of the three, who hadn't yet grown massive muscles like the other two, but he still looked strong enough to take them on.

Jorunn began to laugh. "Oh my god, it just hit me. Saint Nik and all his bullshit about us Aussie girls being obsessed with Australian actors, and he totally got owned by a wolverine. Not quite Hugh Jackman, but…oh shit. Karma bit that thieving arsehole on the arse, all right."

Freyja blinked. "Nik was stealing stuff?" She'd heard rumours about artefacts going missing, but Karl had just dismissed it as poor attention to detail when they were packing up, as it was mostly small stuff that was easy to misplace. Had Nik somehow masterminded the theft of the ice mummy, too?

The helicopter pilot had said he'd had to go to the hospital first with Nik, before he'd brought the ice mummy here. That meant the pilot had to be in on it. Then again, he'd said something about cleaning the helicopter, so maybe if the ice mummy had been taken out and switched while the cleaning was going on, without the pilot noticing, he might be as innocent as she was.

Which meant...the body might have been stolen before it even arrived at the lab. Maybe that block of ice she'd taken to the necropsy fridge had been just that – a big block of ice, with nothing inside. Well, except maybe that spear...

Jorunn nodded. "Yep, and he tried to pin the whole thing on me. He was smuggling stuff back in the waste containers. Thor and Sibyl confirmed it, but Karl didn't believe me until he went through Nik's pockets, in the coat and pants he left behind. Quite the haul of Viking valuables. I heard when he arrived in hospital, the police handcuffed him to the bed.

I bet he loved waking up like that."

Freyja slumped. If Nik had been unconscious all the way from the dig site, he couldn't possibly have been involved in the body theft. Wouldn't have even known the body existed.

And yet…if someone had switched one ice block for another, it was still possible that she'd never received Karl's ice mummy, and being snowed in here actually proved her innocence, because there was no way she could have gotten out, let alone taken a non-existent body with her.

But the police would never believe it. Not unless the body turned up somewhere else. And she had no idea where it might be, except that it definitely wasn't here.

She reached for her muffin, only to find her plate was empty. Would Sibyl mind if she had another one? If she was going to prison on Monday anyway…

"Hey, it's nice thinking about Saint Nik getting a bit of justice and all, but remember the real reason we're here," said the youngest man, whose name Freyja still didn't know, though he was looking pointedly at her now. "We're here to talk to Odin."

The big daddy of the Norse pantheon? Freyja couldn't have heard right. "Who?"

"Odin. Karl's ice mummy. That's what we've been calling him," Jorunn said.

Fuck. Freyja had thought the police were what she'd have to worry about, but the way these four crowded around her, radiating expectation? They were going to kill her when they found out.

She swallowed. And told them.

The man whose name she didn't know spread his hands wide, as if asking the universe for patience. Or maybe even Odin himself. "What do you mean, Odin's missing?"

THIRTY-FIVE

Freyja had no words left. She'd told them everything, even if she hadn't mentioned her suspicions about Olaf or the helicopter pilot. Well, and the bit about her own personal history. Nik had probably already told them, like he'd told everyone else at the university, and if they didn't know, they soon would.

So she said the only thing she could think of: "I'll show you."

She marched to the necropsy lab, where she had to swipe her passcard twice, her hands were shaking so badly. She wouldn't have minded keeping it a secret for another few days, before her life as she knew it ended, but when had she ever gotten to choose what happened in her life? People just barged in and fucked things up whenever they pleased, and she had no control over anything. She was supposed to have pancakes for breakfast this morning, and instead she'd had a couple of muffins. Good muffins, sure, with weird jam that worked in a way she didn't quite understand, but definitely not pancakes.

She shoved the door open so hard, it bounced off the wall, but one of the men caught it in time before it could hit anyone. She'd be grateful for that later, but right now, she just didn't care any more. How could she, when everything was so fucked up?

Freyja wrenched the fridge door open, and flung that against the wall, too, where it caught on the hook that was supposed to hold it open. So everyone could see how fucking empty the fridge was. Much like her future.

She couldn't even bring herself to look at the empty mortuary trolley, where a solitary spear swam in a pool of melted ice.

"What happened to his clothes?" one of the men asked.

Sibyl coughed. "Well, that's the thing about ice archaeology. The ice melts and refreezes, depending on the weather each year, so while some things stay frozen pretty much from the moment they hit the ground, other things melt out, or get moved, depending on what the ice does. So if something falls into a glacier, it's likely to get crushed by all the ice moving over the years. Sure, it's slow, but that's a lot of pressure. Even modern bodies don't last long, or so I've heard. Whereas if a shirt falls off a sled into the snow, like the tunic Nik found, and almost instantly freezes, and it stays there like that for a couple thousand years, the first time it defrosts…well, it's like when you freeze food. It stays fresh."

"So, you're saying the ice in his clothes melted, and they wore out, but then the ice froze around him again?" one of the men asked.

"Yes, but…"

"That's not possible," Freyja interrupted. "Human flesh is every bit as fragile as clothing. Sometimes even more so, depending on what bacteria is present. If we had bones encased in fragments of clothing, that would make sense. Or leather clothing, protecting the body, maybe. But for the clothes to completely disintegrate and leave the body intact…that's just not possible. Now, if the body was buried naked…" She took a step closer, so she could see the body that she couldn't quite believe lay on the trolley, like it had never gone missing at all.

Which made no sense. She'd seen the empty trolley. Olaf had seen the empty trolley. He'd even picked up the spear, which this body was holding across his torso, like some medieval knight with a sword. Not that it hid much, him being naked and all. The weapon between his legs looked more impressive, especially given how cold it was in here. When he was alive, women must have absolutely flocked to his bed, with a cock that big. One of Olaf's ancestors, for sure.

She knew she should grab a pair of gloves, so she didn't risk contaminating the body. But she had to touch it with her bare hands, to know it was real, and not a hallucination.

Freyja reached out, her fingers hovering over the spear, then moving down, past his private parts, to…wow, he still had hair on his legs. Sling a towel around his waist, and he might have been Thor, just stepped out of the shower.

Finally, she lowered her hand, resting her fingers on his calf, which seemed safe enough. She was surprised at how cold he felt, then mentally shook herself. This was an ice mummy that had lain in the ice for hundreds of years, before arriving here in the lab fridge…well, she wasn't exactly sure when he'd arrived here, seeing as this was the first time she'd actually seen him, in the flesh, so to speak, instead of encased in ice, but in order to stay so well preserved, he'd have to have been somewhere cold in the interim.

She wanted to ask him where he'd been. What sort of life he'd lived, before he ended up in the ice, but mostly…where he'd disappeared to over the last week. She wanted to look him in the eye, and tell him he was as fucking selfish as Amal.

So without really thinking about it, she moved along the trolley, so she was level with his head. Automatically, she reached for his throat, to check for a pulse. She wasn't surprised she didn't feel one. It was silly she'd even bothered to check. Someone this cold was definitely dead.

She took a deep breath, fixed her gaze on his face and said…

"Oh fuck. Olaf?"

THIRTY-SIX

"Who's Olaf?"

"Oh, he was the maintenance man here. He didn't even last a day."

"Is working here that bad?"

"No, he arrived at work, only to get a message that his wife had been in an accident, so he had to go to hospital. A rock climbing accident, where she'd fallen and broken her arm, and she needed surgery. So he went to hospital to hold her hand and take care of her and stuff, except one of the nurses caught this virus. You know, the one everyone's going crazy about right now, but she didn't know she had it, so she gave it to…well, pretty much everyone. Olaf. Olaf's wife, plus a whole lot of other staff and patients. So they quarantined the whole hospital. And just when you think they're finally going to be allowed to go home…Olaf gets sick. Really sick. Like, complications with the virus and gets sent to Intensive Care sick. So his wife's the one holding the phone, sending messages to the lab group chat. I checked this morning, and it looks like he's finally been allowed to go home, but no way has he been cleared as fit for work. Especially a physical job like maintenance. But the thing is, you can't fire someone for getting infected, and the university can't hire someone new to replace him, even if Karl weren't up in the mountains. So Olaf is the maintenance man we don't have. We have his uniforms, his security pass…pretty much everything, except the man they're meant for."

"Does he look like Olaf?"

"How should I know? I never met him. But he's wearing Olaf's uniform, with his name on it, so it's safe to say they're the same size."

"So why didn't you tell her?"

"Because there never seemed to be a good time to tell her my last memory from more than a thousand years ago was having my heart cut out by a witch who put a spell on me, before burying me alive."

"That's…that's your last memory? Not the things Erik said about me?"

"Erik was a bag of wind who loved to talk, even when any sane man had stopped listening. I refused to break bread with him, for I knew I would never keep the food down. A cup of spiced wine from his healer was all the hospitality I could stomach in Erik's hall. Unlike some."

"There was a reason for it, I promise you."

"Of that, I am certain."

"I was trying to poison Erik's sons. Like

he'd killed my family, I wanted him to suffer, too. Before I killed him."

"A pity you did not succeed."

"I do not know whether I did or not. The poisons were ones that act slowly, over several days. By the time the sons died, we were already cursed."

"Have you heard anything of Erik since you have awoken?"

"Only his witch, and the abomination. Her wolf man."

"I have heard her voice in my dreams. She calls us, tries to awaken us. Does she not know we are already awake and bound to protect already?"

"She seeks us still, so perhaps she does not. That is why we are here. Together, we may defeat her and the abomination, and remove this curse upon us."

"I cannot help you. I am bound to protect her, and in order to do so, I must return to my slumber. If she does not have a body of a man from our time, she will face a trial for theft."

"That won't work, you know. Awake or asleep, you're not human any more, and we have technology now that will show that. But no one believes in curses or magic or any of this stuff any more, so no one will believe the findings. She'll look like a fool. All of us will."

"So…we need another body. One that isn't mine or yours or Thor's. Do you know where the rest of our men were buried?"

"No. The witch took them away. She said I would see them again when it was time to lead them to victory in Erik's name, and not before then."

Someone exploded into laughter. "As though you would ever serve Erik!"

"There are many things I would do to preserve the lives of my men, though I feared he would not honour the bargain. To see you here, to hear your voices again, brings joy to my heart I never thought to feel again."

"Look, the blossoming bromance here is really lovely, and I think we should absolutely come back to it later, probably with popcorn and drinks, but didn't you just say that you're all going to stay cursed unless you can defeat this witch, and to do that requires all three of you, and you boys need the three of us, because you'll never survive in this time on your own."

"Ye-es…"

"But in order to make sure you have three of us, and poor Freyja doesn't get arrested, we need to find a body in the ice. The sort of body Karl has only found once in a decade of searching, and then, it was just you."

"I will find one."

"We don't have a decade. We only have two days, and with the sunlight thing, it's only really two nights."

"One day and a night is all I need. A day of searching the ice, and a night to fly the body back here."

"You have to make sure the body is old enough. At least a thousand years, maybe more. Perfectly preserved, so it looks like it's just sleeping. And no nazis."

"What in the gods' name is a nazi?"

"Well, he likely would have been wearing a symbol like this on his clothing somewhere."

Several of them burst out laughing. "That is Odin's family crest. If he'd been wearing clothes, you would have seen that symbol on him."

"So what are the chances of finding the dead body of one of Odin's relatives in the ice?"

"Very low. We burned the bodies of our dead in my family, and I was the last one left when we fought against Erik."

"So, leave anyone wearing this symbol, or in modern clothes you don't recognise. And steer clear of the witch. If you fly back tonight, you'll have all of tomorrow to search, and return the following night, before the police arrive. Do you think you can do it?"

"For Odin and his beloved, I will. But first, I must return your wife's brooch. Thor, do you have it?"

"Sibyl said she had to put it somewhere safe.

Can you get it, Sibyl?"

"Hush. She stirs."

Freyja wanted to believe she was dreaming, but she knew those voices too well. Most of them, anyway. Even if nothing they said made any sense.

Maybe she had suffered a bad head injury when she'd lost control of the scooter, and none of this was real. The whole week with Olaf and the ice mummy going missing. She'd open her eyes and…

Olaf beamed at her. "How are you feeling?"

She squinted at him. "How are you not dead? You were cold, just like a cadaver, and naked…" Now he was wearing his overalls again, with his name on the breast pocket and everything. Like she'd imagined everything. "Can you look in the fridge and tell me if the ice mummy is where it's supposed to be?" Because that would solve all her problems. Well, most of them. She'd still have a head injury, but the healthcare system here in Norway was every bit as good as the one at home. She wouldn't have to go to prison, and she'd never eat another pineapple pizza again. But maybe that stuff with the jam…

He frowned. "Loki will see to it that you have your body before the police arrive."

Loki? The man who was going body hunting was called Loki? No. This was a bad idea. Freyja heaved herself up, off the table and onto shaky legs. She had to get to the fridge, to see for herself.

She made it to the fridge, and even managed to open the door, but she had to hang on to it, because her legs threatened to give out underneath her.

The empty mortuary trolley stood there, just as it had all week. No water now, but that spear was there, like the corpse had forgotten it when it had gotten up and walked out.

"Olaf…"

His hands rested firmly on her hips, supporting her. "My name is Odin. I probably should have told you sooner, but it seemed such a small thing, when it was more important to ensure your survival."

She smacked his hands away. "Oh, and while we're talking about small things you should have told me, what about your wife? Didn't you think it was important to mention you had one of those?"

He sighed. "I did have a wife. She died a long time ago."

"Before or after your son died? Or did you lie about that, too?"

"Actually, I do not know. I had a wife and two sons, and she died defending them when our home was attacked, and I was away. When I returned, they were all dead. My whole family."

And just like that, her anger dissolved. Poor Olaf…Odin, or whoever he was. To lose his whole family in one night… "I'm sorry for your loss," she whispered.

"It was a long time ago. More than a thousand years, if I read your history books right. I mourned them, as was proper, as we all did. Then I set out to seek vengeance, which somehow led to me arriving here, and meeting you. It is fate," Odin said, holding his hands out to her.

Freyja didn't take them. "You expect me to believe the body in the ice was you? People don't sleep for a thousand years and just wake up, ready to rescue people and have sex all night. That's not medically possible. You'd need plenty of live, oxygenated blood cells to get an erection, for a start. And English didn't even exist a thousand years ago. I barely understand Shakespeare, and that was only four hundred years ago. This is insane. You are insane. I must have hit my head, because none of this makes sense. I must have imagined you, and the others…"

"Sibyl and Jorunn are from your time, while Thor and Loki are from mine. You can speak to them all. They will confirm that all I have told you is true. They came here to stop you from using science to find out what we are."

Not human. That's what Jorunn had said, hadn't she? He wasn't human. None of the men were. She was almost afraid to ask, but she was also more afraid of what might happen if she didn't know what kind of creature she'd slept with, believing he was a man, when he was something else entirely. "What are you?"

"We called them draugr, in our language. I think in yours the word is gargoyle. The dead who are not dead, protectors bound by magic to answer the call to defend the land on which they are buried, and those who dwell there. You summoned me to save you that night in the snow, and again tonight. You also have the power to send me back to sleep, when I have served my purpose, as I was when you saw me there." Odin pointed at the trolley.

Her hand shot out, before she could really think about what she was doing, and grasped his outstretched arm. His flesh was as warm as hers, maybe even warmer, like he was alive, not dead. It felt as yielding as hard muscle, not...not...

"This makes no sense. How can you be dead, but not dead?"

Odin shrugged. "A witch laid a curse upon me. I know many things, but the ways of witches are beyond all I have learned. Much like your electricity, I fear. My body is living stone. My heart no longer beats and I no longer need food or drink or air to breathe, but the spell gives me the strength I need to defend you, and the knowledge to understand your words, though they were unfamiliar to me. Even my manhood is made for your pleasure. As a human man, never have I known such stamina, and everything that I have, everything that I am, is all for you. You summoned me from my slumber to serve you, and I delight in doing so." He dropped his voice to a low growl. "Especially when you take me into your bed."

Freyja felt her face grow hot. She didn't know where to look. She'd slept with a man who was really a monster. "I thought gargoyles were big and ugly, with wings and horns and things," she blurted out.

Odin bowed his head. Freyja blinked, and

the man she'd known was gone. In his place stood a horned, winged demon. A demon with Odin's face and even his eyepatch.

"Fuck!" she breathed, backing up until she hit the wall. She didn't dare take her eyes off the creature.

"But you see, I am yours to command. And you fear me in this form, while you wish to fuck my other one." Before her eyes, he transformed back into a man. "So this is how I appear to you, so that I may better serve you."

"Which one is really you?"

Odin gestured at his body. "This is what I looked like as a man, in my time. The curse allows me to transform into that creature, so that I may better protect you. Thor tells me our wings are strong enough to carry not just ourselves, but a chosen companion as well. That is how he and Loki brought their wives here, and how Loki will transport the body back, when he finds it."

Freyja just shook her head. "I'll believe it when I see it." And maybe not even then.

THIRTY-SEVEN

While Odin had slept, power had returned to the chamber where he and Freyja had first made love, so she insisted on moving her mattress back there from its present place in the scriptorium. She also insisted she did not need any assistance from him, but this part he intended to ignore.

Now he had nothing to hide from her, he seized the mattress and transported it directly to her room through the walls, without having to manoeuvre it around corners and through narrow passageways, as they had before. It took several minutes before she joined him in her chamber, during which time he'd already set the mattress back on the bed frame.

What he'd give to lie her down and make love to her on this bed again…but he feared that would not happen now, for he'd seen the revulsion in her eyes when he'd appeared to her in his accursed form. He'd not been able to suppress a shudder himself when he'd seen his own monstrous reflection, so he could hardly blame her.

So he forced himself to bow and say, "Let me know if you wish for my assistance with anything else," before he departed. He found the others in the feasting hall, clustered around a table. When he sat down, Loki pushed a small box toward him.

"Frigg's brooch," he said. "The girls say that you must return it, as it is a priceless artefact, which they promise to keep safe for you. I maintain that it is your property, therefore it is your choice what you do with it, just as Thor's hammer belongs to him."

"Sibyl may study my hammer for as long as she wishes, as long as it is within arm's reach for me to use it to defend her, as necessary," Thor said.

Thor would never have been parted from his weapon in the past. He must truly love this woman to surrender it to her, something Odin would never have believed possible in a man who loved battle more than anything.

Odin had always envied Thor for his clear, uncomplicated views on life. Thor went for what he wanted without worrying about consequences, or whether he might not achieve his heart's desire. He kept no secrets, and Odin was fairly certain the man was incapable of lying.

Even now, in a world so alien to their own, Thor had met a woman, fallen in love with her, and persuaded her to marry him. No wonder Odin envied him even more now.

Thor would never understand his relationship with Frigg, or why Odin had withheld the truth from Freyja.

But it was time to come clean. She deserved to know everything. Not just about the curse, but about Frigg, and all the things that had led up to this moment.

Odin scooped up the box. "If you have need of me, you will find me in Freyja's chamber," he said.

The door was locked, so he stepped though the wall. She was sitting on her bed, staring sightlessly at the wall, too deep in thought to notice him at first. Then she blinked, frowned, and said, "Didn't Vikings do privacy in your time? You could have at least knocked."

Odin perched on the corner of her bed. "I feared you would not have allowed me to enter."

"Well, yeah. Privacy. I'm still trying to get my head straight with…all this. You. Them. Learning I had sex with a thousand year old man. That's a hell of an age gap, and while I was falsely accused of necrophilia in the past, now I might have actually done it, and I'm not sure I know how to feel about that. Worse, I liked it, so what does that say about me?" There was an edge of hysteria in her tone, and Odin knew that was his fault. He had driven her to this, and he owed it to her to help her make sense of it all.

"You told me about the shameful things in your past. About the man whose selfish actions drove you to flee your home. I told you a little about losing my son, and you were…kind. Sympathetic. Things I did not deserve, for I did not tell you everything. For a start, I did not tell you about my wife."

"Yeah, you really should have. I mean, if the wound's still too fresh, I get why you might not want to talk about her, but I deserved to know."

Odin nodded. He opened the box and laid it on the bed. "This brooch belonged to my wife, Frigg. It was her dowry, a gift from her mother. She was wearing it when she died, and

I wore it every day until the night I was cursed. Your people found it in the ice, near where I was buried."

Freyja picked up the box and peered inside. "It's beautiful," she breathed. "Is that amber and gold?"

"Yes. Such a jewel would have fed my entire village for a year or more, and there were some long, cold winters that Frigg offered it up in order to do so, but I would never allow it. It was hers, and I intended to lay it on her grave, buried in her ashes, once I had seen justice done for her death. Alas, I failed, and my shame brought me to you. My own men do not know what I am about to tell you, for I fear they would desert me if they did. I have already lost what little regard you might have had for me, but you deserve to know the whole tale. You only saw the monster when I showed you my cursed form, but I fear the monster that lies inside has hidden within me for much longer than that. Will you do me the honour of listening to my tale, though I know

I do not deserve it?"

Freyja folded her arms across her chest. "If it explains how a man can sleep for a thousand years and wake up in my lab. Not because you deserve it, but because if I end up going to prison because of you, then I deserve to hear this."

Odin took a deep breath, and began.

THIRTY-EIGHT

"My father was the chief of our village. We lived on a narrow strip of land between the mountains and the sea, which gave our people access to unique trade goods, as well as making it difficult for raiders to reach us. This did not stop us from sending raiding parties up into the mountains, to raid hunting camps or herds sent up for summer pasture, but most of the time we spent our time fishing and farming, and we sent out trading caravans to other villages. We were known to have superior warriors, and my father insisted that if I wished to be the chieftain after his passing, then I would need to learn to be the best warrior, as well as the best trade master, so I was sent out often.

"One particular mission, my father had made it known that he wanted me to find a bride, a girl who would bring wealth and connections to our village, so everywhere I went, the other chieftains threw their daughters and unmarried sisters in my path. Most of them were comely and welcoming enough, but none of them distracted me from what I felt was my true quest: a successful and profitable trading mission.

"Until I met Frigg. She was slightly older than me, and unlike the other girls, she slammed my jug of mead down in front of me with a scowl and said she'd rather marry my horse than any man, and she'd thank me if I told her father so, for he would not listen to her. I laughed, and offered to share the jug with her if she would tell me why she was so fond of horses.

"It turned out that she had met one of the southern missionaries, the men who claimed there were not many gods, but only one, and that under his worship, women had formed into communities of learning where they did not marry, and could live their lives as they pleased, for the good of the community. I was fascinated by her story, particularly as my father had insisted I learn to speak and write Latin as well as Norse, and I had never met a woman who shared my love of learning."

Freyja blew out a frustrated breath. "So you fell in love with her on the spot and got married?"

Odin laughed. "Wherever did you get that idea? No, of course not. We drank mead for most of the night until we were quite drunk, and I woke up in the back of the cart, with the sun high in the sky, swearing I would never drink again.

"Some months later, after arriving home at the end of a successful trading expedition, my father fell ill and died, and my people voted me into his place. The first snows had fallen and we were busy preparing stores for winter, when a girl in rags entered the village. She had been badly beaten, and she refused to see a healer until she had spoken to me.

"Of course, I agreed. I offered her hospitality, as was proper, and asked her who had done this to her. She looked me squarely in the eye and said, 'You did.'

"I had never beaten a woman in my life, not even a shieldmaiden when we were out raiding, so I was about to send her away, when she told her tale. You see, this was Frigg, and sometime that night, drunk on mead, we had shared a bed, and she had fallen pregnant. She had never been with a man before or since, so she knew the babe was mine, and she'd told her father so, but he called her a whore, beat her, and cast her out. Her mother had given her a small bundle of clothes, some coins and this brooch, but with winter coming and no idea where to go, this had not lasted long. In desperation, she had come to me – a woman who would rather marry my horse than me.

"She had tried to go to the Christian community, but they had turned her away, for they only accepted scholars with a large donation of wealth, and they preferred virgins, not fallen women with children underfoot. So one night with me that I did not even remember had cost her the dream she cherished – and I owed it to her to make reparations.

"I offered to let her stay here the winter, until she gave birth to our child, and then on our next trading mission, I would take her to the convent myself, with a large enough donation to see her working in their scriptorium for the rest of her life, as she wished. She accepted my bargain…until the day after our babies were born, for she was carrying twin sons. I do not know if it was her love for Vali and Vidarr that made her stay, or her belief that I had no idea what to do with two newborns, but we struck a new deal. She would marry me, and remain my wife until our sons were grown, and then retire to the convent. I, in turn, would teach her what I knew of Latin and runes, so that she could teach them to our sons.

"So Frigg became my wife, and to everyone in the village, we were a couple in love. We never fought, and when I was away from home, she took charge of the village, and no one, not even me, disputed her right to do so. She was the best chatelaine I have ever known, and even in the longest, coldest winters, we never went short.

"But she was never truly my wife. She never shared her body with me again after that one night, and she made no secret of the fact that she preferred it was I was away from home, whether raiding or trading, as long as I was bringing things home to make our village more prosperous. She was our chieftain, more than I was, but because she was my wife, and she was good at it, no one every stopped to question it, least of all me. I was grateful for the good care she took of our sons, and our village.

"So when the attack came, none of us expected it. Most of our best warriors, myself included, were away, and Frigg was left to fight Erik's men off alone. Or Erik's draugr, as I learned later. Too late, as fate would have it, but that part of my tale comes later. Erik's army slaughtered everyone. My family. Thor's family. Everyone who was left behind. Yet they did not behave like normal raiders, taking our stores and valuables, for even Frigg's body still bore her brooch, stained with her lifeblood.

"Some years before, the same had happened to Loki's village, and he'd come to us for help, making him the sole survivor of the attack. It had made no sense to me at the time, but now I know it was draugr, commanded to kill so that Erik could take our lands for his own, I begin to understand. Too late.

"Our remaining men vowed revenge, and I

could not deny them. Frigg and my sons deserved vengeance as much as anyone. So we repaired the village as best we could, and mourned our dead, all the while, planning how we might attack Erik, and see that he paid for his crimes against us.

"With Loki's help, for he is an expert scout without peer, I began to build a picture of Erik's tactics. His draugr attacked from the sea, walking out of the water with little warning, so if we had any change of defeating him, we needed to do so in a place where he did not have draugr nearby. The only place where this was possible was a summer pasture camp in the Jotunheimen Mountains, where Erik had been born and raised. This village was called Utgard, and while he did not return there every year, a raid there would be a strike to his heart, so we waited until we knew he would be there, and we sneaked in through the mountain pass.

"When we came close, I sent Loki out scouting. He went, but he did not return. I knew this could mean one of two things.

Either Erik's men had captured him, or they had not, but they were too close to our encampment for him to return without giving away our position. Either way, we had lost the element of surprise. Erik knew we were coming, and our only hope was to kill him and as many of his men as we could, before we joined our families in Valhalla. I knew when we left the pass, that I was leading my men to their death, but I also knew that if I gave them the choice, they would decide to die gloriously in battle, as they would have died defending their families. Thor, warrior at heart though he was, offered to lead the charge, in honour of his sister. How could I refuse?

"I saw my men cut down. Even Thor, who battled like a berserker, was overwhelmed. When there was nothing left but dead and dying men on the field, Erik had his men haul me to his village, where he put his torturer to work on me. But what is pain when you have lost everything, and all you want to do is die? When the man plucked out my eye, I begged him to take the other, too, so that I would no longer have to look upon my failure.

"It was Erik who stopped him. Erik, who showed mercy. He said not all of my men were dead, and if I was the leader he'd heard I was, he needed me to command his army, and if I agreed to serve him, he would allow my remaining men to live."

Odin let out a bitter laugh. "A braver man would have spat in Erik's face, and demanded death. But I had lived with Frigg, who spoke of self-sacrifice, as she had done for our sons. For my men who remained...I chose slavery, so that they might live. I did not believe Erik would hold to our bargain, for I knew the man who had murdered my children could have no honour to speak of, but if he broke his word, then I would not need to hold to mine. And if but one of my men lived – stubborn Thor, or wily Loki – then perhaps vengeance would still be served. Not at my hand, but no less deserved.

"And so I allowed his healer to dress my

wounds, and as she was also his witch, I allowed her to cast her spell over me. Only when it was done did I discover that she intended to curse Thor and Loki, too, and Erik would force me to watch, taunting me that he would kill them anyway, and that there was nothing I could do, for the curse already bound me to him.

"I dare not tell Loki or Thor about the bargain I made, or ask for their forgiveness. We all deserved to die that day, and it was my cowardice that cursed us all. Worse, is that I do not regret it, for when I awoke, instead of commanding armies in Erik's name, my first task was to save you, before taking you to bed.

"The moment I saw your face, I knew I was in love, and when your body joined with mine…neither Valhalla nor Frigg's Heaven could compare to the joy I felt. It was the best night of my life, only surpassed by the other nights I have spent in your embrace since."

Odin took a deep breath. "I am a fool and a failure, as selfish as the man who drove you away from your home to here. If not for the curse, I would have been nothing more than a corpse in your cold storage chamber, something for your science to find answers from. Now, because of me, you may face justice for a crime you never committed. I cannot even begin to think how to compensate you for what I have done to you, and yet when I think of you, it is not guilt that overwhelms me, but love, and how grateful I am for the days I have spent with you. I am sorry, Freyja, for having wronged you."

Without waiting for a response, he rose and turned, as if to walk out of her room, as easily as he'd stepped into it.

Her mind whirling, Freyja didn't know what to think. "Wait," she said.

Actually, she didn't want to think at all. So she threw her arms around his neck and kissed him instead.

THIRTY-NINE

Odin could scarcely believe Freyja had touched him, let alone kissed him, but her lips were still soft against his, as undeniably real as everything else he'd told her. How could she touch him, knowing the truth about him?

"I'm a monster," he tried to remind her, summoning the horns and wings so that she would see him again and remember. "A selfish monster responsible for getting everyone around him killed. I've ruined your life just by being near you. I will…"

"Shut up and kiss me. Better yet, fuck me. I've spent the last week trying to resist you because you're my employee, and then I thought you were dead, and now you've just told me the most tragic, fucked up story I can barely even imagine, where a hug and a bit of sympathy are just not going to cut it, and THEN you tell me our first night together was the best night of your life? And the ones after that, too? Because they were mine, too, and I've just spent the last hour trying to come to terms with the fact that not only am I in love with an undead monster, but every time I see you, I want to rip your clothes off and have you. Repeatedly. Even as you're telling me every chapter of your tragic tale, half my mind is fantasising about how much I want you to fuck me, like your fool of a wife never did." She stripped off her clothes, leaving them in a puddle on the floor, and wrapped her legs around his hips. "We're both failures, and everything falls apart around us. But right now, it's just the two of us here, and no one else matters. I want to feel your monster cock deep inside me, Odin. What do you want?"

The desire in her gaze burned him to his very bones. He couldn't refuse her, even if he wanted to.

So he slowly peeled off Olaf's clothing, until he stood as naked as his beloved. Beautiful, soft Freyja, the woman he didn't deserve. "I want to hear you scream. I want to hear you scream my name, as you take my cock."

He lifted her up, pinning her to the wall, before he impaled her.

"Oh, Odin. More, please!" she begged. Her legs tightened around his hips, urging him deeper.

Gods, she felt good. So tight around him, clenching down hard like she never wanted to let go. Then she grabbed his horns in her hands, and guided his mouth to her breast.

Sweetness and softness and…yes, she was screaming, screaming his name in absolute ecstasy, but he couldn't stop.

FORTY

By the time they were done, Freyja could barely walk, so Odin carried her to bed, and tucked her beneath the blankets.

"More, please, Odin. Make love to me some more," she mumbled, wrapping her hand around his cock.

Odin laughed softly and leaned forward to kiss her. "Later, beloved. When you have rested. It is late, and humans need sleep. When you wake, I will be ready for you. I will always be ready for you. I am your monster."

"Mmm. My monster," she murmured, as her eyes drifted shut.

Perhaps he shouldn't have pounded into her so hard, so that she'd scream louder. Then she might not have tired so quickly, and they might have made love for longer. He swore he'd keep the pace slow and steady next time, so that they'd have all night.

Next time, and the one after that.

It took all his willpower to leave her chamber and return to the others in the cafeteria. Except the only person left there was the blonde girl, Jorunn.

"Where is everyone?" he asked.

"I imagine Freyja's asleep, or you'd still be pounding the walls. Sibyl and Thor are busy breaking the bed, and Loki and I would be doing the same, except he left as soon as it got dark, so he could steal a body for you." She gestured toward his horns. "I take it you told her everything and it went well, then? Unless I missed the argument and what I heard was make up sex."

Before, when he was married to Frigg, talk of sex had always made him uncomfortable, because he knew he'd have to lie. Now, though…

Odin allowed himself a satisfied smile. "I believe she is pleased with me, yes."

"I sure hope so, because that's some seriously fucked up shit you pulled. Faking your own death. If Loki tried that with me, I'd pull all his feathers off."

It took Odin a moment to realise what she'd said. "He told you his secret?" Loki must intend to marry the woman, then, for he'd never told anyone else. Odin only knew because Loki had come to him in animal form when his village was under attack.

"Which one? The shapeshifting, or the illusions? Or just magic in general? I've got to admit, the night he made himself look like me still makes me shudder. I have nightmares that he'll do it again one night when we're doing it, and put me right off." She shuddered. "He flew back as a falcon. He said it'd be faster. Thor wanted him to take his time choosing a body and to come back tomorrow night, but he promised me he'd be back by dawn. He'll be pissed if Thor and Sibyl break the bed before we do."

"How long until dawn?" Odin asked. Slumbering in cold storage, and all his time inside this building, he didn't know what time it was.

Jorunn glanced at the thick bracelet encircling her wrist. "A couple of hours at most, I think. Maybe less. The sun rises early this time of year."

Odin blinked. "I thought it was winter, with all the snow on the ground."

Jorunn grinned. "Nope. It's the height of summer, not long past the solstice. Climate change has really messed up the weather. Early ice melt meant we got to go out to the dig site early, only to get buried in a summer blizzard. Can't even blame a volcano for this one. All the solar panels in the world won't save us, though I suppose we can hope." Then she shook her head. "Sorry. A lot of scientific advancements have happened while you were asleep. I should probably see if there's a science history channel on the internet or something that'll help you catch up."

Odin wasn't sure what she was talking about. "The solar panels on the roof help to regulate the weather?"

Jorunn blinked. "Well, maybe, if you consider reducing fossil fuel emissions to be helping, even if it's only a little. I didn't even know we had solar panels out here. I mean, it seems a bit counterintuitive, what with all the snow and all. Where'd you learn about them?"

"I read the maintenance manual for this place, then every book in the library," Odin said. "Is it true that nazis, the people who wore my family crest, killed six million people?" He could barely believe there were that many people alive in the world, let alone dead.

"History isn't really my forte. I'm a biologist

by trade, so I know more about reindeer and thylacines than concentration camps. But I did hear that the numbers in the official history books are a gross underestimate. I met a Polish girl once who used to be a guide at one of the camps, and she said it was more like twenty million."

Odin couldn't imagine those kind of numbers.

Loki stumbled into the cafeteria, looking absolutely exhausted. "Wake up the others, so you can tell me where to put the body. I've left it outside in the snow, but I'll need to get it inside by dawn, and that's not far off."

Odin held up his hand. "Let them sleep. I shall show you, and if Freyja wants you to move it or do anything else with it, she can tell you in the morning."

FORTY-ONE

Freyja woke in a warm, snug bed, with a body pressed up against hers. Odin, just as magnificent as she remembered. No horns this morning, though. But his cock was hard and ready, reminding her how much she wanted more of him. Especially if the police would be here to arrest her tomorrow morning. This might be the last chance she had to have morning sex with him ever.

"Ah, you are awake. The others will be

pleased. They have been waiting to see if you approve of Loki's find."

Loki…hadn't they sent him looking for a body?

Suddenly she wasn't so interested in sex any more. Cadavers did do that to a person.

"Can't we just stay in bed a little longer?"

"If you approve of what he brought, then I will be able to warm your bed every night, for as long as you wish."

"Forever." The word was out of her mouth before she'd thought it through, but she knew it was true.

"Then let this be the first morning of forever," Odin said, pressing a kiss to her bare shoulder.

Freyja swallowed. If by some miracle, Loki had found a second ice mummy at the site, old enough to be from Odin's time, or earlier, she would be safe. She could stay here, with a job, a home…and Odin.

It would indeed take a miracle, but for all that, she was willing to hope.

So she showered and dressed with her usual morning efficiency, and followed Odin to the lab.

"Finally!" Loki said, throwing his hands in the air. "It's too late for me to take it back today if you don't like it, let alone find another one, but you wanted a body that's from our time, who did not serve Odin's family, and is very well preserved. This one is all three." He looked smug.

"Show her, then," Odin said.

"If you would open the door…"

Freyja swiped her pass card and let them all into the necropsy lab. She was sick of the sight of this fridge, but she opened the door anyway. The sooner this was over with, the better, because then she could have breakfast. Autopsies before breakfast. Always. Because things could get way too messy if you did them the wrong way around.

This time, there was a body bag on the trolley, zipped up all the way. Freyja blew out a breath. "Couldn't you have opened it up?"

Loki shrugged. 'There was no point, if you wanted me to take him back again. So I left him in the bag."

Body shopping. The man had gone body shopping for her. If she thought about it too hard, she'd go mad.

So she donned a pair of gloves instead, and unzipped the bag. The body was still frozen, with a thin layer of ice crystals frosting his clothing, which she gauged to be made of wool. Not modern, at least, and the lack of buttons was promising. He wore no gloves, and his hands were in remarkably good condition. More like a recent cadaver than one that had been in the ice for a millennium. Her belly began to twist uncomfortably. Maybe this was a murder victim after all.

She glanced down the body, and her heart sank. The hilt of a knife protruded from the body's belly, in the middle of a dark stain on the man's tunic that might have been blood. She reached for the knife.

"Walrus ivory. This was the eating knife of a

rich man," Loki said.

"How do you know?" Freyja asked, almost afraid of the answer.

Loki shrugged. "Because I once challenged its owner to an eating contest, and won."

Freyja froze. "You know this man?"

"I might have spoken to him once. Maybe. But I know his kind."

Realisation dawned. "But you know the man who killed him."

Another shrug. "I know the man who owned the knife. But I don't think he stabbed him, on account of being already dead." Loki reached into the bag and pulled out a stone tablet, covered with Viking runes. "He came with a warning."

Odin took the tablet from him. "Here lies Orm the traitor, who betrayed his brother and his king. He poisoned the two princes, before he stabbed the king. When he tried to claim the throne, justice was done. He is buried here without honour, for he had none," he read. He touched his eye patch. "This is the torturer who took my eye."

"And here I thought you were wounded in battle. Well, the joke's on him, because I know for a fact he didn't poison Erik's sons," Loki said. "But if he was the one who killed Erik, then perhaps I'll let him go down in history as the man who murdered his sons, too. It looks like they buried him alive for it. A fitting end for this bastard. Almost as good as being raped to death by randy reindeer. Or walruses. Now walruses would make things really messy…"

Freyja stared at the man. What was wrong with him?

"Loki, shut your mouth. There is a lady present," Odin said.

"Yes, Odin."

Freyja took a deep breath, trying to steady herself. Whoever this man had been, he was from the Viking age. A fitting ice mummy for Karl and his students to study. No matter what crimes he might have committed during his life, his presence here was about to save her from being arrested.

"We need to get him out of the bag, and onto the table," she said.

With Odin and Loki's help, they soon had him ready for study, with the runestone carefully placed above his head. It would not have fitted on the table with Odin, but Orm was considerably shorter than even Loki, the smallest of the three men.

Finally, Freyja could breathe. She peeled off her gloves, then washed her hands thoroughly, before leading the way out of the lab.

"After the week I've just had, that body in the fridge is enough to make me want to have champagne. But as I drank it all…perhaps a celebratory breakfast will do."

Loki waved his hands. "Yes, you go do human things. I promised Jorunn we would break the bed before breakfast, so I will go wake her."

Freyja looked at Odin. "Should we follow him, to make sure she's all right?"

Odin smiled. "Just as I am your protector, he is hers. As long as he is cursed, he cannot hurt her. Besides, Jorunn is made of the same stuff as the shieldmaidens of my time. It is Loki who must watch himself with a woman like that."

FORTY-TWO

"If they are on foot, then they will arrive here tonight," Thor said. "We must have a plan."

"How could they possibly know where we are? No one knows we're here except us. They couldn't possibly have followed us here unless they could fly, in which case, they'd already be here. So what makes you think they'll come here?" Sibyl asked.

"Because even the dullest witch can do a

scrying spell to find what they are looking for," Loki said.

Jorunn brightened. "So you can tell us where they are?"

Loki winced. "I can try, but unless I recognise the place, it still won't help."

"But we still must have a plan," Thor insisted. He turned to Odin. "What shall we do?"

Odin sighed. That was the problem, wasn't it? Thor and Loki, like the rest of his men, would follow him anywhere. They'd even followed him here. But then, just like now, he still hadn't truly known a way they could win.

"What do we know? The witch is coming, with the wolf man. He is her protector, so any threat to the witch will be met with force from him," Odin began.

"I will fight Fenrir. I have my hammer, and I am stronger now. There are no other warriors here to distract me. This time, I will be victorious, leaving the rest of you to deal with the witch," Thor said eagerly.

"Do we know what powers the witch has? She is a healer, and she cast the curse on us. What else could she do?" Odin asked.

Loki spread his hands wide. "Her mother was a powerful enchantress, whose spells kept me captive in Erik's longhouse while the battle raged outside. If she learned magic from her mother, and inherited even part of her power, there is no telling what spells she might cast."

"So we make sure we meet them outside. I don't want any of you destroying my lab," Freyja said.

Odin nodded. "Yes. If there is a battle, it must be outside in the courtyard. We three warriors will meet them, while you women…"

"Here it comes. Scratch a man and you'll find the misogyny," Jorunn said, setting her hands on her hips. "I've got news for you, big Viking warrior. Us girls aren't hiding anywhere. You three might be good at whacking things with swords and hammers and axes, but you know bugger all about this time, or the world as it is now. If they know even the slightest bit more than you do, you're fucked. You need us."

"Loki," Odin began, appealing to the man for help.

Jorunn just shook her head. "If you're about to tell him to control his woman, I'm about to dump this can of coke in your lap. You might be made of living stone, mate, but this is acid, strong enough to clean coins. How long do you think Freyja will stay with you if I melt your cock off?"

"You would use sorcery on me?" Odin asked.

Jorunn shrugged. "Actually, it's just basic chemistry. Or alchemy, for the medieval misogynists in the room."

Loki just stared at her like a lovesick fool. "Marry me," he said.

Jorunn considered for a moment. "If we survive this encounter with a thousand year old witch and her immortal werewolf, I will."

Loki's grin widened. "So, while Thor's playing with the wolfman, we distract the witch. If she bites her lip, distract her before she can cast a spell. Blood fuels her magic, so whatever you do, don't make her bleed. When the wolf is down, we fan out and surround her. She can't take all of us at once, and we convince her to tell us where Erik is, if he's still alive, and maybe even break the curse. Freyja, is there a particular place outside we should choose for our battlefield?"

Freyja nodded. "The courtyard between the loading dock and the outbuildings, next to the helipad. It's still covered in snow, so…maybe we could distract the witch by throwing snowballs at her? Odin?"

Loki burst out laughing. "Did he tell you about the time he knocked out a reindeer with a snowball? He stole it from me and everything. I already had it half tamed, and he just came in and wham! It woke up harnessed to his sled, and that was it. It was Odin's pet reindeer after that." He shook his head. "Maybe that'll work on the witch. If all else fails, knock her out with a snowball, Odin."

Odin buried his head in his hands. "This is a terrible plan."

Thor clapped him on the back. "Then let's go outside to the courtyard and think of a better one!"

They all trooped down to the loading dock, where the girls donned their snow gear and the guys stood around waiting, not sure what to say. As if their easy camaraderie as brothers in arms had been left frozen in the ice while the centuries passed.

Yet they were the same people. Thor tossed his hammer from one hand to the other, with a vague smile on his face. Loki licked his lips, intent on some idea that he would surely tell them when he was ready. And Odin…

His eyes darted from his men, to the women. Sibyl looked like a girl in her padded jacket, with little more than her eyes showing. Jorunn flicked switches on the wall, while Freyja was still reluctantly tugging on her jacket, after taking forever to pull on her boots. While the others looked like they wanted to be here, she was putting on a brave face, her eyes darting back down the corridor, deeper inside the building.

Odin moved to her side. "You don't need to do this, you know. You can stay inside, where you'll be safe."

Freyja just gave him a funny look. "I'm not going to run and hide. I was thinking of going back for the first aid kit. In case someone hurts themselves, it'll save time if we already have it here."

"You're not afraid?"

"I'm afraid someone will get hurt. Magic and monsters might be more than I can understand, but I'm still a doctor, and I know that if someone can get injured, they will, and that I should be prepared." She wet her lips. "I'm going to get the first aid kit. I'll be right back, okay?" She hurried off.

Jorunn pressed the button to open the roller door, then looked around. "Where'd Freyja go?"

"She went to get something. She said she'd

be right back."

"Well, I hope so, because it looks like we have visitors," Sibyl said grimly.

FORTY-THREE

Odin might have mistaken the pair for people of this time, for they wore modern garments, though styled more like those of his time. Her tunic glowed a dark blood red in the bright lights beaming across the courtyard, above polished leather boots. Over it all, she wore a dark woollen cloak that seemed to glitter like the night sky above. She looked like just a girl, younger than Freyja and her friends, until her gaze met his and recognition sparked.

She inclined her head. "Well met, Jarl Odin."

Odin was at a loss – he did not remember the witch's name.

Thor, like a good brother in arms, came to his rescue. "You are an abomination, and you do not deserve to live! I, Thor, Hymir's son, so vow and I will not rest until you are dead!" He flew across the courtyard and slammed into the witch's companion, knocking him into the snow.

The fight was fast and furious, for though Thor wielded his hammer and more than once Odin heard the sound of the hammer head cracking what could only be bone, the wolfman sprouted fur, fangs and claws, all of which he used liberally on Thor.

Snow flew up in clouds, obscuring the fight for minutes at a time, until the combatants appeared, roaring and snarling at one another, before tumbling to the ground out of sight once more.

"You have to stop this!" Sibyl insisted, grabbing the witch's shoulders, for the girl had come to stand beside the lab door like the rest of them, to get out of the way of the fight.

The witch shrugged. "They are men, and men will always fight. Especially when there is honour at stake. There is no sense in trying to stop them, until they are finished with this foolishness, or one of them has won."

"I can do this all day!" the wolf man snarled.

"And I can do this all night!" Thor growled back.

An almighty crack sounded somewhere in the snow, and both men roared in response.

Sibyl sniffed. "So much for being a powerful witch. If you won't stop this, I will." She charged into the snow before anyone could stop her.

Another deafening crack, a ringing clang, and then a man's scream: "Sibyl!"

FORTY-FOUR

When Freyja reached the loading dock, the door was wide open and everyone was gone. "I said I'd only be a second," she grumbled as she left the gurney on the dock, with the first aid boxes stacked on top of it. Why had no one thought to put a trolley in the first aid room? The moment she got back to her laptop, she was going to order one.

She trudged down the steps to the snow

dusted veranda. "What have I…"

A loud gonging drowned out her words. A sound that could only have come from something hitting that fucking sundial. Hard.

Then a man's scream: "Sibyl!"

Freyja didn't think. She broke into a run.

The first thing that came into view was the plinth that had once held the sundial. One piece was still stuck to it, but the rest of it had broken into smaller pieces, the largest of which was sitting on Sibyl's chest, where she lay on the snow.

She gasped for breath, her lips beginning to turn blue, while two men stood over her.

"You did this!" Thor howled.

"You broke that thing, not me!" the stranger shot back.

Fucking idiots. "Move," she ordered, shoving them out of the way so she could kneel beside Sibyl. It was as bad as she'd suspected. One of the jagged metal pieces of the sculpture had pierced Sibyl's jacket, and likely her flesh beneath, too.

Sibyl stretched out bloodied fingers toward Freyja. "Help," she mouthed, but no sound came out.

"Someone get me the first aid kit. Bring it right here, now!" Freyja shouted.

She had to get the sundial off Sibyl, but right now, that was what was sealing her wound. If Freyja judged wrong, and it had pierced the girl's heart or an artery, she might bleed out. But if she didn't, she was going to suffocate. Fuck.

If only she could call an ambulance and get the girl to hospital. But they were still snowed in. Not even a helicopter could land. This was all up to her.

The first aid kit arrived and Freyja ripped it open, laying it out on the snow. She grabbed a handful of gauze packages, ready to rip them open so she could apply pressure on the wound the moment they removed the sundial.

Unless…

If she had an open pneumothorax, she'd need to dress the wound immediately, and get an air tube in there. She'd need a sterile environment for that – it wasn't something she wanted to do out here in the snow.

"Get me the gurney. Bring it right here, lay it down beside her," Freyja said, pulling on gloves. She prepped two sets of dressings – a pile of gauze she could apply pressure to, in order to staunch the bleeding or an airtight one to stop air getting in. The stretcher landed in the snow.

"Right, you two, grab that metal thing, and I'm going to count to three. On three, you're going to lift it off her. One, two, THREE."

Sibyl groaned in agony as the sundial came free, but Freyja already had her scissors out, slicing away Sibyl's jacket so she could see the wound. Oh, thank fuck…open pneumothorax. Freyja grabbed the correct dressing, taping it on three sides, just like she'd practiced.

Only Sibyl still couldn't breathe. Her lips were definitely blue now.

They had to get her inside.

"Right, you and you, muscles. On three,

we're all going to slide her onto the stretcher, and then you're going to carry her inside. Ready? One, two, three."

Thor and the other man obeyed, and the snow seemed to part like the Red Sea for them as they glided through it to the loading dock, where they stuck the stretcher back on the gurney.

Thor helped her push Sibyl into the first aid room, where Freyja grabbed an oxygen bottle – the one thing she hadn't bothered to bring with her earlier – and fitted the mask to Sibyl's face.

"What are you doing? What is that?" Thor yelped.

The last thing Freya needed were hysterical family members getting in her face. "Someone get him the fuck out of here so I can focus on my patient."

'Sibyl! Sibyl!" Thor roared as the other men dragged him out.

Freyja glanced down at Sibyl again, only to find another woman's hands on the wound.

Bare hands, no gloves, not even a squirt of sanitiser. "Get your hands off my patient," Freyja growled.

The girl just smiled at her. She said something Freyja didn't understand then closed her eyes, her hands still on Sibyl's chest.

Freyja reached out to grab the girl's arm.

Only to have her own arm grabbed by a hand with fur and claws.

Freyja blinked. The strange man stood beside her, radiating menace.

Freyja didn't care.

"Look, I need to take care of my patient. If you want to help, scrub up and sanitise, and then maybe I'll let you pass me stuff." Not bloody likely, but it would keep them out of her way for a moment.

The girl said something else, then bit her lip and touched Freyja's forehead.

Share your knowledge with me, she seemed to say, though Freyja was sure she hadn't heard the words at all, before her mind went mad, flipping through memories like some sort of movie montage. Her pracs in the respiratory ward. Page after page from her textbooks. Dissecting endless cadavers. Rotations in the Emergency Department. More textbooks.

And then…the image of what was inside Sibyl's chest, beneath the dressing. The jagged wound, her lung collapsing in on itself. Like someone had stuck an endoscope in there, but they didn't have that sort of stuff here. Yet as Freyja watched, the wound began to heal. In the darkness beneath Sibyl's ribs, her lung swelled as she inhaled.

"Fuck," Freyja breathed.

The strange man was shouting something, but Freyja ignored him. She had to save Sibyl. She had to…

"It's all right. She's a healer." That was Odin, standing in the doorway.

"Yeah, I know all about medieval medicine. Butchers full of bullshit, the lot of them. Can you get someone to call an ambulance? If I'm lucky, I might be able to stabilise her, but I need to get these two out of here first. I told them, but either they don't understand or they don't care that a girl could die if they don't."

Odin spoke, and the girl replied.

Odin sighed. "She says she is healing your friend, using your knowledge. You must be patient and quiet, because this requires focus and a delicate touch, with just the right amount of power. When she is finished healing her, she would like to borrow your books."

Freyja just shook her head. "If this girl can save Sibyl's life, she can have all of my textbooks to keep. Or, better yet, I'll buy her a set, brand new, in whatever language she does speak, seeing as English evidently isn't one of them."

"Latin and Old Norse, I'm afraid. Like me."

Freyja stared at the girl. "She's a gargoyle like you?"

"No, she's…she's the witch who made us into gargoyles. And him into…whatever he is." Odin gestured at the strange man with the hairy hands.

The girl said something, then looked

expectantly at Odin.

"She says she's finished healing your friend. Now, she needs to rest, and eat."

Freyja nodded, then turned to her patient. Beneath the oxygen mask, Sibyl's lips were losing their bluish tint. She peeled back the wound dressing, only to find no wound there any more.

She looked up to find the girl's knowing eyes on her. The girl inclined her head, which Freyja took to mean, "You're welcome."

"She says she hopes you have plenty of food, because after that, she could eat a whole dragon," Odin said.

"Definitely not a gargoyle, then." Freyja led the way to the cafeteria.

FORTY-FIVE

While the women ate their meal, Odin stood against the wall of the feasting hall, waiting to see if he'd be needed as an interpreter. The wolf man imitated him, though now he looked fully human again, as he watched over the witch. He definitely took his bodyguard duties seriously.

A hand tapped Odin's shoulder.

Loki. "Can I talk to you for a minute?"

Odin's eyes never left the women's table. "Sure, but it'll have to be here. I'm not leaving Freyja alone with that wolf man here."

"It's the witch I'm worried about. If she does anything to Jorunn…"

Loki in love. Odin never thought he'd see the day.

"What do you wish to discuss?" Odin asked. He hoped it wouldn't be marital advice.

"It's about the things Erik said, and what happened when I left you all in the pass to go scouting. I need to know if you believed him, that I was a traitor."

"Erik was a bag of piss and wind. I'd sooner believe what came out of a wolverine's arse than anything that came out of his mouth. I know you. You'd happily turn Thor's hammer into a fish, or my spear into a sausage, but you would never turn on your brothers in arms. Every prank you played, you were only too happy to admit you were responsible, so we could all laugh with you. Yes, you have your secrets, as do we all, but you never kept them from me."

Loki breathed out a sigh of relief. "You don't know how happy I am to hear that. I sneaked into Erik's camp in the hope of killing him, but the witch caught me, and kept me from returning to you. I didn't even know you'd survived until the night she cut out our hearts. I figured if I was the last of us, I owed it to you all to stay and find a way to kill Erik, and take away his family. His sons…"

Odin's eyebrows rose. "So it was not the traitor Orm who poisoned them, but you?"

Loki ducked his head. "Fate played a part. It was almost as if fate wanted those men to die."

"Many men died that day. I still do not understand why we were not among them," Odin admitted. "Truly, I believed we were all marching to our deaths. That is why, when you went out scouting and did not return, we marched anyway. Because I knew Erik's men would be waiting, but I knew our men were not willing to wait any longer for vengeance. Even if it killed us all." He sighed. "The only traitor on the field that day was me, for it didn't matter what I did. I would betray my men by leading them into battle, or I would betray the memory of those who died by running away. Only to be captured by Erik, and offered a choice – the lives of my remaining men, if I agreed to serve him. I believed he would let you live, not that he would turn you into a draugr, as he had me." Odin shook his head. "He was a faithless liar to the last. I hope that man Orm did kill him, and that his death was slow. He does not appear in the history books of this time, so it seems the world has forgotten Erik, while we still live on."

"It is done!" Thor roared as he stomped into the feasting hall.

"What have you done now?" Loki asked, eyeing Thor's snow covered boots.

"The strange metal thing that slayed Sibyl is no more. I have shredded it into pieces so small, they scattered on the wind!" Thor said.

"You've destroyed the sundial?" Freyja said,

half rising from her seat.

Odin winced. "He will see it forged anew for you, I promise."

Freyja sat down again. "It doesn't matter. I never liked it anyway. I'm sure it was insured. We'll say it was carried away by the storm. I'm sure the university can afford to commission a new one. Or get some new art to put in its place."

The witch set down her can of beer and belched. "Now I have eaten, I will have some answers. Tell me: where is my father, Erik of Utgard?"

Loki and Odin exchanged glances.

"Well…" Loki began.

Odin cleared his throat. "We believe he was stabbed by a man named Orm."

The witch's eyes blazed. "Where is he? I shall slay the man myself."

"It might be a bit late for that," Loki said.

"Take me to him!" the witch insisted.

Freyja rose. "What's her problem now?"

"She wants to see your ice mummy," Odin

said.

"As long as she doesn't touch him, I guess we can do that," Freyja said.

In the cold storage room, it was not Orm's body, but the stone tablet that held the witch's attention. She even laughed. "It is true. The man had no honour, yet my father tried to give me to him. Fenrir was right to take me away, though I did not believe it at first." She tossed the tablet back onto the table. "What will you do with him?"

Odin translated her question for Freyja, who replied, "We will scan him, and learn as much as we can from him. Scholars will study his body, inside and out, so that we may increase our knowledge about the people of your time."

When the witch heard this, she only laughed harder. "Oh, that is a fitting fate for a traitor. Not even as a corpse will he know rest!"

"I'm sorry about your father, and your brothers," Odin said. Not that he felt Erik was any great loss to the world, but he had been the girl's father. And to lose her brothers, too…

The witch waved away his sympathies. "I had many brothers. My father lay with a different woman each night, and had many sons. All of them wished to prove themselves worthy of his notice, so they took many risks during battle, drinking far too much jusquiasmus than was good for them. There was no antidote if they took too much, which they often did. They lived and died as warriors, and the next day, Father would find more to fill their places. He never bothered to claim any of his daughters, except me, because I had magic. He was my father, but he only cared that I was useful to him. First as a witch, then as a wife to keep Orm loyal, which must have failed when Fenrir took me. Come, we must drink to justice, which finally caught up with the traitor!"

When the witch was seated in the cafeteria once more, with a fresh beer in her hand, Odin dared to breathe a sigh of relief. Freyja's ice mummy was safe, and so were they, for the moment.

"But none of you have answered my question. Where is my father, Erik of Utgard?" the witch demanded.

FORTY-SIX

"Erik of Utgard was buried far from here, in a lavish boat burial, together with a runestone that told the story of his conquests. It mentioned the pass where we have been digging as the route to Utgard, which is why I joined the expedition," Sibyl said hoarsely, as she staggered into the feasting hall, using the wall for support.

Freyja jumped to her feet. "You shouldn't

be up!"

Sibyl waved her away. "I am fine. She healed me." She pointed at the witch, then switched from English back to halting Old Norse. "I owe you a debt of gratitude, Lady…?"

"My name is Astrid, and your answer is payment enough. My creatures were responsible for your injury, so it was only fitting that I heal it. And I am repaid. Did you see my father's body, lying in state?" the witch asked.

Sibyl shook her head. "There were only bones left, and I have seen pictures of them. I can show you, if you like." Thor moved to support her, but she flapped a hand at him. "Just help me sit down, then go get my laptop. And you are going to promise me never to fight with that bloke ever again, or so help me, you are going to learn about divorce."

Thor's eyes widened, and he hurried out.

Sibyl turned her hard gaze on Astrid. "Now, you and I need to get one thing straight. That one is my creature. He's handfasted to me, and if you think you can just wave your hands and make him follow you like a well-trained puppy, we are going to have words, and they will not be nice ones."

Odin tensed, ready to step forward to defend Sibyl in Thor's absence for saying such unwise words to a witch.

Astrid tilted her head. "You woke him. That is why they were not in the mountains, where I left them. Thor answered your call, and resisted mine. Is it the same for the others? Do they serve the other women?"

Sibyl swallowed. "I think so, yes. My cousin Callie sent me some information about gargoyles, and how they are protectors. She even sent me the spell for creating them, though I couldn't imagine cutting out anyone's heart." She shuddered.

Astrid's smile was tight. "It is quite messy, especially as you cannot reach it without breaking some bones. Very unpleasant. If my father had not commanded it, I never would have done it once, let alone many times."

"How many?" Odin asked.

"Too many," Fenrir said. "I was her first, and I will protect her to the last."

Odin digested this for a moment. He knew it was unwise to ask, but he had to know. "With your father and brothers dead, all of these creatures answer to you now. What do you intend to do with your draugr army?"

Astrid shuddered. "My father's army, not mine. I must release them."

Thor walked in and handed a strange, flat device to Sibyl. "Who else are you holding prisoner?"

Astrid closed her eyes. "Countless draugr, gargoyles, protectors cursed to answer my father's call. I must release them."

Fenrir stepped forward. "I shall help you, and protect you, as always."

"But I should release you, too."

"I asked for this. I swore to protect you, and I will. We stand together. But these others…you should release them. Let them seek happiness with the mortal women of this time."

Thor stepped up to stand right in front of Fenrir. "You only want that because you want me weaker, so you can win."

Fenrir shrugged. "I take no pleasure in fighting. I am Astrid's loyal bodyguard. I fought to defend her, and at her father's command. If Erik is truly dead, then I only answer to Astrid now, and she was most displeased at having to heal you the first time. If you are no threat to her, then I have no argument with you."

"You killed my sister."

Fenrir frowned. "I have never killed a woman in my life. Boys, maybe, when they take up weapons against me. There was one boy in a village on the coast once…ferocious fighter. A little like you, for he would not surrender, even when he knew he had lost. With his last breath, he demanded I send him to Valhalla. Now I think of it, he had a weapon like yours, too, though he could barely lift it."

"My sister, dressed in boys' garb," Thor said

through gritted teeth.

"If I had known, I would have spared her. I am sorry for your loss. But I can assure you, she earned her place in Valhalla. Perhaps even among the Valkyrie."

"Yes," Thor said.

"Give up the grudge, or get a divorce, Thor. I'm not going through that again," Sibyl said. "Shake hands with the werewolf, or whatever he is."

Thor squeezed his eyes shut, then held out his hand. "I, Thor, Hymir's son, swear I will never harm Miss Astrid, as long as you will swear never again to harm my Sibyl."

"It is agreed," Fenrir said, gripping Thor's arm in the way of warriors.

"What about them, then?" Sibyl asked.

Fenrir frowned. "What do you mean?"

"She said she'd free them. Slavery is illegal in this time, and you have no idea how much trouble you'll get into for it. So, free them. Take the curse off Thor and Odin and Loki. Do that, and I'll show you those pictures.

Maybe even hook you up with some of my contacts who might know where you can find other gargoyles, too." Sibyl said.

Fenrir's frown deepened. "You wish to hook me like a fish? Or Astrid?"

Sibyl just shook her head. "Some things just don't translate. Astrid, will you set these men free?"

Astrid smiled. "Yes. For to undo my father's work is to set myself free, also."

FORTY-SEVEN

"Doctor Freyja Valdis?"

Freyja forced out a smile as she held the door open wider for the small crowd outside. "That's me. Please come in."

Ingrid, the only woman among them, shook hands with her before sidling inside, followed by the two police officers and an older man Freyja assumed was the university photographer.

"Can you show us where the body was found?" one of the police asked.

Freya couldn't help it – she laughed. "I can show you pictures of the dig site in the mountains where it was found, and the preliminary x-rays I took this morning, now the power's back on, but if you want to see the dig site, you'll have to wait for Jakop and his packhorses, and when they do their next supply run in a few days. Unless you can get approval to send in another helicopter, but you'd best talk to Karl, the expedition leader, before you do that. Conditions up there can be very different to the weather we get here."

The police officers held a muttered exchange in Norwegian that Freyja didn't understand. Finally, one of them nodded. "Show us the body, then."

Freyja led them to the necropsy lab, swiped the door open, and headed for the fridge. She threw open the door just as she had for Thor, Loki and the others, but this time, she knew exactly what she'd find. Orm had not moved since she'd x-rayed him, and Astrid has assured her that unlike Odin, he was definitely dead.

Ingrid's photographer was in there first, snapping photos of the body in the fridge, while the police officers pulled on protective clothing. Freyja just stood back and watched — she had a forensics degree herself, so there was nothing the police would discover that she didn't already know. Orm belonged in an archaeology lab, not in the hands of a police coroner.

Finally, one of the men peeled off his mask, then his gloves. "Not a police matter. You can keep him," he said.

So they'd missed a few details, had they? "That's what we thought. Even if he was murdered, or executed, we estimate it was over a thousand years ago, so there isn't much chance of catching the killer. The ultimate cold case," Freyja said.

The talkative one stared at her. "Murdered? How can you be sure?"

Freyja pulled on her own pair of gloves,

then delicately pulled aside a fold of Orm's shirt, revealing the knife buried in his guts. "Well, there's this, which indicated he probably died a slow, agonising death, and there's also the runestone that was found with him, that describes the crimes he was executed for. An example of early Norwegian justice at work."

Both officers grinned at that. Then they were asked to pose for pictures, though with their faces hidden, before they insisted they needed to get back.

After the police left, Freyja wheeled the body out into the necropsy lab, where the photographer could make use of better lighting and more space to take more photos and video of the body, before she returned it to the fridge and had to answer a lot of questions from Ingrid on what she'd learned about Orm.

Freyja found herself repeating plenty of variations of "I don't know yet" until Ingrid was finally satisfied, and put her laptop away. If any of the reporters who received the press release wanted to ask further questions, they would contact Freyja, Ingrid said.

Freyja wished she could refuse, but Karl's discovery deserved all the press coverage she could get. Even if it was Orm, and not Odin.

Speaking of Odin…where was he?

FORTY-EIGHT

A white, boxy cart, much larger than the vehicles Freyja's visitors had arrived in, trundled up the road, past the main building, and round the back, to where the courtyard was still filled with snow. A man got out of the cart and swore.

"Who is that?" Thor asked.

Sibyl shrugged. "I have no idea. He looks like he's headed for the shed where the waste barrels are kept, but they don't get collected until the end of the season. It's cheaper for the university to only pay for one truck trip, because the truck needs special waste permits. There aren't any signs on the outside of that van, so I doubt he's here officially. You should go ask him."

"Me?" Odin asked.

"Sure. You're Olaf, the caretaker, or at least that's what it says on your overalls," Sibyl said.

But Freyja had said to stay out of everyone's way, until the police left. She wouldn't like this.

"He's wearing the same thing," Odin said, pointing at Thor.

Sibyl raised her eyes to the ceiling. "Fine. Both of you go and ask him, then. Ask if he needs any help."

Odin trudged into the courtyard, almost wishing Astrid hadn't broken the curse, so that the snow wouldn't slow him down like it did now. Did they not have snowshoes in this time? He hailed the man.

The man definitely looked furtive then, like

he was looking for a quick escape.

"I'm Olaf, the caretaker here. Can I help you?" Odin asked, hearing Thor's footsteps behind him. "This is Thor." For Odin might be able to maintain a pretend identity, but Thor was too forthright for such things.

The man bared his teeth in a smile that definitely didn't reach his eyes. "I'm Thrym, here to pick up the waste. It's usually in this building." He pointed at the shed Sibyl had mentioned.

"Of course, of course! We'll help you carry the barrels across the snow. You should have come later, when the snow melts, and it would be easier. But it doesn't matter. We will help you," Odin said, heading for the shed. He lifted the nearest barrel, and carried it out. "Where would you like me to put it?"

Thrym's eyes widened. "Oh, I don't need all of them. Just the marked ones. Someone else will come for the others."

"What sort of mark?" Odin asked, examining the barrel. There were many marks around it.

Thor emerged from the shed. "Like this one?" His barrel bore his family rune.

Thrym looked relieved. "Yes. The ones with the old runes on them. Nik's little joke."

Thor's face turned thunderous. "You are only taking those marked with ancient runes? Not the rest?"

"Yes." Thrym opened the rear door of his cart. "You can put that one in here."

Odin set his barrel down at Thor's feet. "I'll do it. You put this one back inside, with the rest. I'll meet you back in the shed, and show you which ones we want."

Thor looked like he wanted to argue, but he'd always been as loyal and obedient as he was forthright. He might not like it, but he obeyed.

Odin set the barrel inside the cart and hurried after Thor.

"You can't let him take these! He's a thief!" Thor hissed the moment Odin entered the shed.

"I know. You and Sibyl told me they hid your hammer in one of these," Odin said, lifting another barrel.

"You don't understand! Sibyl told me to put it back in a barrel — that barrel, the one you loaded into his cart!" Thor said. "We can't allow him to take it!"

No, they could not.

Freyja had said the police, people whose job it was to mete out justice in this world, were here. She'd feared they would accuse her of theft. But if there really was a thief here...

"I have a plan. Pick up one of the marked barrels, and follow me," Odin said.

"But..."

"I said follow me!" Odin shouted.

Thor muttered under his breath, but he did as he was told.

Odin climbed up into the cart. "Now, pass that up here to me."

"We can't..."

"I said lift up that barrel!" Odin roared.

"I heard you! I just don't think we should!"

Thor shouted back.

"Give it to me!"

"You're a fool!"

"And you're an idiot! Give me that barrel!" Odin bellowed, loud enough to wake the dead.

Thor lifted it, but was reluctant to let go. "This is wrong!" He slammed the barrel down on the ground, so the lid flew off. But Thor didn't notice – he was too busy climbing into the cart. He grabbed the barrels already inside and proceeded to toss them out onto the ground, too.

"This is a valuable historical artefact, and it should be locked away safe, not smuggled out to be stolen!" Thor boomed, picking up his hammer from the smashed barrel.

"Everybody put your hands up!"

Thor grinned, lifting his hammer in both hands…only to drop it on Thrym's feet.

Odin had never heard such a shrill scream from a man before. But anyone who tried to steal Thor's hammer surely deserved their fate.

"What's going on out here?" That was

Freyja, looking as thunderous as the sky on the night they'd met. Sibyl and Jorunn were with her.

"These men appear to have been fighting," one of the policemen said. "We heard shouting, and then saw this mess."

Odin moved closer to Freyja, his hands still held high. "This man said he was here to collect the waste barrels. As I am the caretaker here, I came to help him, but the barrel fell and this was inside." He gestured at the hammer that had definitely done some damage to the man's feet.

Sibyl stepped forward. "That hammer should be in the artefact room. You were trying to steal priceless artefacts!" She pointed at Thrym.

"Not me! Doctor Fridolfsen pays me to collect the waste. Just waste!" Thrym babbled.

Freyja folded her arms across her chest. "Nik Fridolfsen isn't in charge here. I am. And I did not authorise any waste collection or movement of artefacts from the facility. Arrest this man as Nik's accomplice."

The policemen looked bewildered. "What about the other men?"

"They are my staff. They were aware of Dr Fridolfsen's arrest, and I'd asked them to keep an eye out for anyone suspicious on the property, particularly if they were attempting to remove anything from the facility. It looks like that's exactly what they did here – tried to stop him from stealing these waste containers that definitely didn't contain waste. Thor? Odin? Is that what was happening here?"

Odin nodded. "Of course, Doctor Valdis. As you see, we were right to be suspicious."

After some arguing, the policemen took Thrym and his vehicle with them, along with a large number of pictures of the broken barrels and artefacts, but none of the actual artefacts, because Freyja was insistent that no police evidence locker was equipped to properly preserve priceless cultural treasures, whereas the facilities at Icelab were designed to do just that. When one of the policemen suggested that the lab might not be secure, she merely shrugged and said the contents of the barrels couldn't have come from inside Icelab, as the barrels were sealed at the dig site and remained sealed until disposed of by the waste contractor, because of the risks of transferring some unknown pathogen from the ice. Even she wouldn't handle the contents of those barrels without a hazmat suit.

The policemen backed off in a hurry, leaving Thor and Odin to clean up the mess, while Sibyl and Jorunn took care of the artefacts. Ingrid and her photographer headed off, too, chattering in rapid Norwegian about the press coverage they hoped to get for this story.

"I can't believe we finally caught them. Such incredible luck that Nik's accomplice came here while the police were here. Karl's been trying to work out how things have been going missing for years now. If Nik had gone to Egypt this year, like he'd originally planned, we might never have figured out it was him,"

Freyja said.

Jorunn shrugged. "Saint Nik probably contacted him as soon as he could, only Thrym couldn't get here until the roads were cleared. If he had gone to Saqqara instead, hopefully his colleagues in Egypt would have found him out before too much went missing…and I've heard the penalties for theft there, especially valuable antiquities, are a whole lot harsher than here in Norway. Oh well. At least he won't be stealing stuff again in a hurry."

"Or the other guy. Did Thor really crush both of the poor man's feet with his hammer?"

"I dropped it," Thor said, looking aggrieved. "I should have swung it at him instead and broken more than just his feet."

"Then you really would have lost your hammer," Sibyl said. "If you'd killed a man with it, the police would have arrested you and taken away the murder weapon as evidence. So it's a good thing you only dropped it. Now, we know it'll stay safe here."

The others headed inside, but Odin and Freyja lingered in the courtyard. The melting snow had washed away Sibyl's blood, leaving no sign of Thor and Fenrir's fight, aside from the broken sundial that Freyja had already informed the university had been damaged by the blizzard.

"Did everything go well with Orm and the policemen?" Odin asked.

Freyja smiled. "Yes, of course. They were just leaving when we heard shouting, and came out here to investigate. You're lucky the police didn't look too deeply into your background. Sibyl said she has a cousin back home who might be able to help you get some identity documents so you, Thor and Loki can pass for modern men. It will take some time, though."

"In the meantime, I will stay here with you, as your maintenance man," Odin declared.

Freyja laughed. "Oh, I hope you'll be a lot more than that!"

FORTY-NINE

Freyja sat down in the cafeteria and opened up her laptop. It felt like forever since she'd last talked to her family, but in reality, it had only been a few weeks. She'd tried calling earlier, but this was the first time everyone's rosters had lined up enough to have everyone home.

Of course, Mum answered. "Hello, darling. How is the iceman doing?"

Freyja blinked. She hadn't told them about

Odin – how could they possibly know?

Fintan's face popped up behind Mum's shoulder. "Mum's been following every news story and article she can find on your iceman since she first saw you being interviewed on the news. Even at my work, people were asking if I was related to you. You're famous!'

Oh, they meant Orm, not Odin. "Well, he's definitely dead. It's still early days yet. Forensics isn't as fast as it looks on the TV programs. Sometimes it takes weeks to get the test results back, and my team here is quite small. When the summer dig season is over, some of the archaeologists will join me, and we'll find out more then, plus write up some papers to put out to all the right journals. So far, all we know for sure is that he was from the Viking era." With Ingrid's help, they'd managed to keep the runestone out of the news coverage, as that's the first thing Freyja and Sibyl intended to write a paper about, linking this discovery with the runestone from Erik's grave that had sent Sibyl to this site in the first place.

"We're so proud of you, darling. I knew you weren't entirely happy in medicine, but I always thought you'd find your feet while you were travelling. I never thought you'd be making historic discoveries over there!" Mum said.

Freyja's heart blossomed in her chest. After so many years feeling she was a failure, it was nice to be praised for once.

Wait…Mum had known she wasn't happy?

"Ugh, enough about dead guys. I want to hear about the hot, live ones. You never did send me any pictures," Kendall complained, dropping to her knees beside Mum's chair.

Mum shot Kendall an annoyed look. "We are all very proud of your sister. She's out there, making a name for herself, instead of chasing men every moment."

"Patients, Mum. Most of those men are my patients," Kendall said, rolling her eyes.

Even from the other side of the world, Freyja knew that was a lie. Fraternising with patients, much like necrophilia, was definitely not considered appropriate conduct for a doctor.

"You speak to your sister. I need to get dinner started," Mum declared, getting up.

Kendall slid into Mum's seat. "Right. I want to hear everything. Please don't tell me you've been so busy with the dead guy, you haven't had time for any live ones. There's no point you going all the way to Norway unless you claim some mighty Viking cock."

Odin wandered into the cafeteria, carrying a plate with a muffin topped with lingonberry jam. "Who are you speaking to?"

"Who is that?" Kendall squealed.

Freyja closed her eyes and took a deep breath. "Odin, this is my sister, Kendall, video calling from Australia, on the other side of the world. She has an unhealthy obsession with men's genitals, as if she doesn't already see enough of them at work. Kendall, this is…"

"I am Odin. My mighty Viking cock belongs to Doctor Freyja Valdis, and no one else."

Freyja wanted to slide under the table in embarrassment.

Kendall let out another squeal. "You have a boyfriend? Does he always talk dirty like that? God, he's hot. Why didn't you send me pictures?"

Freyja began to tell her sister about getting snowed in, but Odin began to kiss her neck, and suddenly, Freyja realised she couldn't continue, without telling her sister everything. Gargoyles and witches and werewolves…much like Odin's private parts, they weren't something she wanted to share with her sister.

"You know what? I gotta go. You have a great week, and give everyone a hug for me. Maybe when the pandemic's over and the borders open, I'll come home again, and Odin can come with me. Meanwhile, we have work to do," Freyja said, letting the cursor hover over the END CALL button.

"But I want to see his…"

The screen went dark.

"So now it's just you and me here," Odin

began.

"Is it? I know Sybil and Jorunn and their boys left with Jakop and the supplies, but I thought Astrid and Fenrir were coming back. They had to go free some more gargoyles, they said."

"She wanted to free all of them. All the men she'd cursed. But she cut out hundreds of hearts, and she said it would take more than a few days to track them down. Especially as they would be walking, instead of using magic to travel, which is apparently what they used last time. Erik wanted to conquer the whole world, and he wanted armies everywhere, ready to help him." Odin shook his head. "We should be grateful to Orm for ending his ambitions when he did. And to Astrid for freeing all the warriors he enslaved. She said she would return to winter with us, before the first snows fell, whether she had finished freeing them all or not. I promised she and Fenrir could celebrate Yule with us. And the others, if they wish it."

Freyja rose. "So it's just us here, and I've finished work for the day. Whatever shall we do?"

Odin grinned. "Well, I have a mighty Viking cock that is eager to do as you command."

"Mm, let's start with your dirty Viking mouth and those calloused Viking hands first, hmm? Then if you are lucky, I'll ride that mighty cock of yours." She'd thought his amazing stamina was part of the enchantment, but he'd since proved that he could happily go all night, even as a man. And what a man.

"I am yours to command, as always, Doctor Freyja."

She held out her hand. "How about we go to bed, then, iceman? I might have spent most of the week working on a different Viking body, but it's yours I want to get my hands on now."

Odin laughed, ignoring her outstretched hand as he scooped her up in his arms. "Then the faster I get you to bed, the sooner I will be able to grant your wish, beloved. All your wishes."

As their clothes drifted to the floor like snowflakes, Freyja took a moment to wonder if all her wishes had already come true. Then she was naked in bed with Odin, and she only had one wish – for more.

So he granted that one, too.

ABOUT THE AUTHOR

Demelza Carlton has always loved the ocean, but on her first snorkelling trip she found she was afraid of fish.

She has since swum with sea lions, sharks and sea cucumbers and stood on spray drenched cliffs over a seething sea as a seven-metre cyclonic swell surged in, shattering a shipwreck below.

Demelza now lives in Perth, Western Australia, the shark attack capital of the world.

The *Ocean's Gift* series was her first foray into fiction, followed by her suspense thriller *Nightmares* trilogy. She swears the *Mel Goes to Hell* series ambushed her on a crowded train and wouldn't leave her alone.

Want to know more? You can follow Demelza on Facebook, Twitter, YouTube or her website, Demelza Carlton's Place at:

www.demelzacarlton.com

www.ingramcontent.com/pod-product-compliance
Lightning Source LLC
Chambersburg PA
CBHW070426170726
48291CB00002B/370